Three Guns Waiting

LUTHER CHANCE

A Black Horse Western

ROBERT HALE · LONDON

ISBN 0 7090 6833 6

Robert Hale Limited
Clerkenwell House
Clerkenwell Green
London EC1R 0HT

*This one for I.J.
in the hope of calmer days*

Typeset by
Derek Doyle & Associates, Liverpool.
Printed and bound in Great Britain by
Antony Rowe Limited, Wiltshire

Three Guns Waiting

Sam Pooley had come to the spread on the Washback to begin a new life – and lost it to the bullets of crazed gunslingers. But that was not to be the end of either the memory of the man, or the fate of the land he left in the care of his proposed bride-to-be. Land baron, Stove Moldoon, had plans to add the spread to his already formidable empire, and was none too fussed about how to set about acquiring it.

If smooth talking failed, there was always the threat of his hard-riding, fast-shooting sidekicks. But nobody, it seemed, had reckoned with the quiet stranger last seen in town on the day they had lain Sam Pooley to uneasy rest. . . .

One

'That's evil-doin' you're lookin' at there, mister. The Devil's work, white hot out of Hell.' The old man spat across the baked noonday dirt, scratched his bald pate and bowed his head as the wagon bearing the single box coffin creaked and trundled by on its slow, measured passage to Boot Hill.

He grunted approvingly to the tall, tanned man standing at his side. Fellow knew his manners well enough, he thought, noting the hat in hand, the lowered gaze. Not bad for a stranger. Cut above most they got through Resolute these days.

He acknowledged the quick, anxious glances of the handful of mourners following the wagon, watched until they were out of earshot then spat again.

'Never gave him a chance,' he murmured, as if assuming the stranger was waiting on him. 'Three shots, one from each of 'em. Clean through the back. Scum!' He hawked in readiness for another fount of well-aimed spittle, eyed a basking fly and drowned it in one. 'I seen some rats, but they don't come no dirtier than Blatch.'

The stranger settled his hat and tipped the brim to shadow the glare.

'Known Sam Pooley since the day he rode in,' the old man continued, squinting into space. 'One time army, he was. Captain Pooley. Settled out the old Fletcher spread start of the Washback. Horse breedin'. Knew his horses too, say that for him. Yessir, fine fella, real manners, and he weren't for no nosyin' neither. Not like some hereabouts.' He glanced sidelong at the stranger. 'Yuh ain't from hereabouts, are yuh? No, figured not.'

The old man thrust his hat on his head, hawked again and spat across the path of a crawling fly. 'Life just ain't one bit fair, yuh know that? Take a fella there like Sam – never did nobody a snitch of harm. Got on with his life out there on the spread, bred the horses, traded honest, lived a decent, upright life. So just what in God's name brings a scumbag like Blatch and his sidekicks crossin' his path for no better reason, savin' that Sam was where he was when he was? Damnit, might've been just about anybody they could've crossed that day – some I might have personally herded their way! Just no damned justice, is there?'

The stranger scuffed the toe of a boot through the dirt.

The old man sighed and ran a gnarled hand over his stubbled chin. 'No justice. . . . Still, it's done now, ain't it? No point bemoanin'. Best look to Sam's horses same as I promised Miss Abi I would – Abigail Grey, that is, Sam's intended. Good-lookin' gal in the bonnet up there on the Hill. Hell, she's cut up real rough.' He sighed again and slapped his lips noisily. 'Tell yuh somethin', mister, if I were twenty years younger, why I'd be out there kickin' the Washback dirt 'til I got alongside them scumbags. Know what I'd do then? I'll tell yuh just what I'd do. I'd plug the three of 'em, startin' with Blatch, and then Riff Stevens and Crazy Man Moon, plug 'em, one by one, square in the back, just like they did for Sam. And then I'd leave the bastards right there for the buzzards. That's what I'd do. Too right I would.'

The stranger grunted quietly.

'But what'll happen?' the old man grumbled on. 'Nothin'! Know what? Sheriff Simmons here reckons as how it's too late to go rattlin' a posse out the Washback. Says Blatch'll be long gone. Huh! Yuh ask me, mister, he's just too damned scared to get to within a mile of the sonofabitch. Lookin' to his own skin, that's what he's doin'. I got no measure to that sorta thinkin'. Yellow-bellied, if yuh ask me. What yuh reckon?'

The stranger raised a tight, narrowed gaze to the gathering at the graveside.

'Well, t'ain't your problem, is it?' murmured the old man, straightening his shoulders from their tired stoop. 'Don't look like it's nobody's problem! I just hope some folk don't get to sleepin' so easy once they finally put Sam to rest. There's them he might come to haunt, eh? Hell, that'd be somethin' to dwell on! Would too.'

The old man squinted into the glare on the Hill and pulled at the loose, floppy brim of his hat. 'Best go pay my respects, I guess. Nice talkin' to yuh mister. Mebbe see yuh around, eh?'

The stranger waited until the old man had joined the silent group of mourners before moving quietly to his horse hitched at the rail on the shaded side of the street, mounting up and riding out on the trail heading north.

He would hit the Washback in under the hour.

TWO

'Well, it's like I say, miss, spread's in good shape and we got some fine stock corralled. Somebody lookin' for a real sound base to get started horse breedin' couldn't do better. Should sell in a month, I'd reckon. Want for me to put the word about? Mebbe out Sioux Falls way? Big money out there. Place is yours to sell, miss. Sam wouldn't want yuh holdin' to somethin' yuh got no taste for.'

The old man called to the team, snapped the reins and leaned to the buckboard's sway and bounce on the rutted trail. 'Yuh only got to say,' he added, with a hurried glance at the woman seated at his side.

Abigail Grey lifted her face to the stream of the cooler plains' breeze, relishing its freshness across her neck where the gown had stayed high-buttoned through the funeral service, happy to feel her long dark hair flowing free of the confines of the bonnet – saddened, as she had known she would be, to sense the tearstains hardening on her cheeks, fearful that her eyes might fill again.

She tightened her grip for her balance against the sway of the outfit and bit quickly at her lower lip. No more tears, she resolved, not for the first time that day; no more gulping on the cynical twists of Fate, the cruelty of it, the loss, the emptiness, the bleakness of the future. No more of any of that. Time had come, in tribute to the memory of the man she had loved and so nearly wed, to gather whatever was left and get to building a tomorrow. Where else was there to go?

She swallowed and cleared her throat. 'Grateful to you, Rawlegs, for standing to me like you have. Wouldn't have gotten through this without you. Know that, don't you?'

'I ain't done nothin' the captain wouldn't have wanted or expected, miss – beggin' yuh pardon for raisin' his memory again – so there's no need for expressin' thanks. You and me known each other too long for that.'

'Mebbe,' sighed Abigail. 'Sam rated yuh some. He ever tell yuh?'

The old man slapped his lips. 'Now when did Captain Pooley ever get to handin' out compliments unnecessary?'

'Not often, but he meant them when he did. "Rawlegs is the best horse-breaker I ever clapped eyes on", he said. True enough. He said it. Reckoned without you he'd never have got the place up and running like he did. Told me so to my face.'

Rawlegs slapped the reins again, but resisted the temptation to spit out his embarrassment. 'Well,' he called above the clatter of the buckboard's sudden bounce, 'that's all as mebbe now, miss. Yuh got to come to some decisions. Captain's will was clear enough: yuh got the homestead and all its contents – personal bits and pieces too – all the stock, and the whole of the spread. That's some land, Miss Abi.

'Far as the swing station at Eagle Springs. Clear up to the mountains west. Down to the banks of the Old Yellow to the east, and a mile short of Resolute back of yuh. Ain't never got to measurin' it out, but I'd sure as hell be lookin' to new boots if I tried!'

Abigail smiled and brushed self-consciously at a stray tear. 'Worth a fortune, I guess.' She sighed again. 'But it's not for measuring in money, is it?'

'No, miss, t'ain't. And the Captain weren't never for discussin' it that way. He saw it different. A home, I guess, though him bein' without family, no kin, nothin' save the military, that ain't so surprisin'. Still. . . . Fetch one helluva price, miss, when yuh come to sellin'. Heck, know what, yuh'll be one of the wealthiest women this side of the Abilene!'

Rawlegs squinted ahead and risked a soft spit from the corner of his mouth. 'Shouldn't have said that, miss,' he murmured. 'Weren't called for and t'ain't none of my business – but, heck, Abigail, I known yuh since yuh were a babe. Watched yuh raised at your pa's mercantile right there in town; stood with yuh when yuh folk passed on in that 'flu outbreak we had in forty-five. . . . We go back far as yuh can recall, and there weren't nobody happier for yuh when yuh said yuh'd wed Sam Pooley than old Rawlegs here. And that's a gospel truth!'

'I know,' said Abigail, laying a hand on the man's arm.

'Tell yuh somethin' else while I've a mind for it – thing's been different and I weren't carryin' the years I am, I'd have been trackin' down them scumbag sonsofbitches did for Sam faster than a louse out of fire 'til I'd seen every last miserable bone of 'em picked clean. Sure I would, just like I was tellin' that fella back there in town.'

'I saw you talking to him,' frowned Abigail. 'Who was he? He say?'

'No, never did. Didn't ask, come to that. Some stranger passin' through, I guess. Paid his respects decent to the dead. Anyhow, gettin' back to what I was sayin' about the spread—'

'You needn't fret yourself another minute on that score,' smiled Abigail, brushing a dance of hair from her cheek. 'I am not for selling up. Sam left the spread to me. It was to be our home. And that's just what it's going to be – a home. You help me, Rawlegs?'

'You bet on it, miss!' shouted the old man. 'There ain't nothin' in the world more certain. Hallelujah – would yuh know, I think we got a future comin' up!'

He snapped the reins and the buckboard bounced like a two-year-old.

The buckboard was still bouncing under the team's licking pace at Rawlegs' urging, Abigail Grey's hair still flying and dancing on the rush of the wind, and the dust clouds swirling thick and fast along the trail out of Resolute heading north for the sprawl of the Washback, when the old man finally swung the outfit clear of the bluff and on to the track to the Sam Pooley spread.

He was all for giving the team the last of their heads for the day. And why not? Heck, there was something to celebrate, worth kicking up the traces and letting down the hair for, but instinct and that niggling prickle back of his neck had tightened his hands on the reins and hauled them short long before he saw the four mounts hitched at the home-stead rail.

'We got company,' shouted Abigail, pointing to the line.

'Yuh expectin' any?' asked Rawlegs, his gaze sharpening on the home, the shaded veranda.

'Not special. Said as how town folk are welcome to look by any time.'

'Them ain't townfolks' horses,' grunted Rawlegs. 'Them's hard riders' mounts.' He noted the scab-bards thick with gleaming Winchesters, the packed bedrolls, worn but one-time expensive saddles.

'Could be some of Sam's old friends looking by,' smiled Abigail, shading her eyes against the glare as the buckboard slowed.

That I doubt, mused Rawlegs, slapping his lips nervously. Horses of that build, looking that good, were hand-picked for their stamina, keeping going through all weathers and any, if not all circum-stances. And you might say the same of the men picked to ride them.

He drew the team to a gentle walk to the side of the main barn, checking instinctively as they passed the corral that the horses there were standing calm and easy.

Abigail fiddled anxiously with the falls of her wind-tousled hair, then with the dusty folds of her gown. 'What a sight I must look for receiving visi-tors,' she murmured, lifting one hand to her dirt-smudged cheek.

Rawlegs halted the outfit, settled the reins at his side and laid a gentle hand to Abigail's arm. 'No rush, miss,' he murmured, his gaze shifting quickly for a movement, the drift of a shadow.

'Can't keep visitors waiting, can we?' began the woman, already making to climb down.

'No, hold it,' snapped Rawlegs, but too late as three men stepped as if out of nowhere from the deepest of the shadows at the side of the ranch and lounged, squinting into the sunlight, like stray cats who had struck it lucky at a pool of spilled milk.

Three

'Howdy,' grinned the taller, younger of the three, his thumbs hooked casually in his belt, one boot beating to a tuneless humming deep in his throat. 'Been waitin' on yuh, ma'am.' He squinted carefully from one eye.

'Easy, miss,' murmured Rawlegs, scanning anxiously for the rider of the fourth mount as Abigail stepped slowly from the buckboard.

'I'm sorry,' said Abigail lightly, 'I don't think we've met. You new around town, friends of Sam's perhaps?' She hesitated a moment. 'You catch us on a sad day,' she went on. 'You see, we've just buried—'

'We know all about Sam Pooley, ma'am,' growled a squatter, thicker man, a growth of black bushy eyebrows hiding the glint in his gaze.

'So you knew Sam?' smiled Abigail.

'In passin'.'

The third man, lean as a post with a thin, bony face where the features seemed to have erupted as if by accident, clicked his fingers as he ran his tongue over his cracked lips. 'Truth is, ma'am, we rode in from the far side of the Washback. Needful way. Yuh heard of Needful?'

'We heard,' snapped Rawlegs, still scanning for the fourth rider.

The bony-faced man glanced dismissively at the old man.

'I'm afraid I don't know the place at all well,' said Abigail. 'Fact is, I rarely have need to go a deal further than Resolute—'

'Nice town, Needful,' grinned the younger man. 'Lots of girls!'

'Lady don't wish to know that,' croaked bushy brows.

Rawlegs slapped his lips. 'Yuh right, she don't. Neither do I. So if you fellas'd like to get to the point of this visit—'

Bony-face man clicked his fingers. 'All in good time, old man, all in good time. We ain't in no hurry.'

Rawlegs squirmed irritably. 'You may not be, but mebbe yuh need remindin' that we just buried a good friend and ain't in no mood for chatty social-izin'.' He glared defiantly. 'Might just add that you happen as of now to be trespassin' on private prop-erty, and the owner of this spread, Miss Abigail Grey here, may not be of a mind to welcome your company.'

'That a fact?' said bony-face, his lips breaking to a baked smile. 'Well, now, ain't we just in luck? Yuh hear that fellas? We ride all that way from Needful wonderin' just who's goin' to take over Sam Pooley's spread and what do we find? We find the new owner right here. A woman. Would yuh know that? A woman – Sam Pooley's squaw comfort, eh? Nice, too.'

'Mind your tongue there, fella,' growled Rawlegs, squirming again.

'I really don't think there's any point in continuing this conversation,' said Abigail, smoothing her hands at her sides. 'You men are welcome to water your mounts—'

'Not so fast, lady,' said bushy-brows, shifting his weight. 'We ain't come all this way to be dismissed outa hand. There's a gentleman here. . . .'

'That'll do, Drakes,' said a voice from the shadows. 'I seen all I want to. Yuh step aside there now. Leave Miss Grey to me.'

Abigail shivered at the twist of cold sweat in her spine.

Stove Moldoon! Rawlegs gulped on a suddenly parched, pinching throat and narrowed his gaze to tight slits on the man facing him. So Moldoon is what this is all about, he thought, settling his hands on his knees; land 'rustling' – give it any fancy-handled legal name you liked, but it came to just that, never no less when you got to it, or more to the point, Moldoon got to it.

Send in the sidekicks, rough up the homesteaders with a few well-chosen words and threats, then, when the fear got a grip, move in to purchase at a price that barely bought the dirt the place stood on. Most folk were just grateful to be alive, settle up and pull out.

That was how the land and cattle empire of Stove Muldoon had come into being over the past fifteen years. And Rawlegs had witnessed every one of them.

'Spreadin' yuh wings some, ain't yuh, Stove?' he clipped hoarsely. 'Don't normally see you and yuh boys operatin' this far south. So what's the big attraction, or need I ask?'

Moldoon, tailored sharp and neat as ever in a quality frock coat, clean shirt, pressed pants and hand-lasted boots, rolled a cheroot through his fingers, placed it carefully in his mouth and lit it slowly, his gaze unblinking behind the thickening cloud of smoke.

'Ain't wastin' no time neither,' added Rawlegs. 'Damnit, we ain't had Sam Pooley buried more than a few hours before you're scratchin' round his bones. Can't yuh let a fella go to his Maker peaceful? T'ain't decent!' He was tempted to spit until glancing quickly at the pale, drawn face of Abigail Grey. 'Lady here ain't for talkin' business. Not today, not tomorrow, and mebbe not—'

'Yuh got an awful lot of lip on yuh there, old man,' drawled Moldoon, shafting a line of cigar smoke. 'Always were lippy, and age ain't improvin' yuh one bit.'

The sidekicks tittered and relaxed on slack hips. Rawlegs slapped his lips.

'Yuh got anythin' to say, Moldoon, yuh'd best say it, and fast. We ain't got the time to be wastin' it.'

'Well, mebbe the lady here might have a say in that. Afternoon, ma'am. Pleased to meet yuh. Miss Abigail Grey, so I'm told.' Moldoon touched the brim of his hat and smiled generously.

'Correct,' said Abigail, stiffening. 'I have heard of you, of course, Mr Moldoon. My pa spoke of you a number of times. . . .'

And not once to say a good word, thought Rawlegs, scowling.

'Mr Pooley, too,' Abigail went on. 'But I really can't imagine why you should wish to see me, or visit here, unless it's to pay your respects to the memory of Sam.'

Moldoon blew more smoke. 'No, ma'am, I ain't payin' no particular respects – me and Pooley weren't exactly of a mind, though I felt a fair disgust at the manner of his killing, same as we all did. But I figure you for knowin' full well why I'm here.' The gaze behind the smoke tightened. 'Reliable word has it that Pooley left yuh this spread. That right?'

'It is,' said Abigail, tossing her hair across her shoulders. 'I am now the legal owner.'

'Congratulations,' smiled Moldoon. 'Yuh got y'self a fair place – mighty fair when you get to it. Handled proper and with the right under-standin'—'

'There ain't no doubt to the handlin' of the place,' snapped Rawlegs.

'Goin' to be too much for you, old man, if that's what yuh plannin'. And no disrespect, ma'am, but I don't figure for yuh copin' on yuh own.'

'Who's sayin' she'll have to?' flared Rawlegs again. 'Miss Abi ain't never been on her own.'

'I'm sure she hasn't,' grinned Moldoon, 'but I'm talkin' man's work here, all day, every day, if yuh goin' to manage the spread proper. Too much for a woman on her own, ma'am, so I suggest yuh give some careful thought to the offer I'm makin' to purchase the place from yuh at a fair market price, cash on the deal, and no messin'.'

'Bah!' spat Rawlegs, aiming the line of spittle to within a hair's-breadth of bushy-brows' boots. The sidekick stepped back, one hand already slipping to the butt of his Colt.

'Yuh gettin' lippy again, old-timer?' droned the younger man. 'Yuh want for me to stitch his mouth, boss?'

'I'll see yuh in hell first!' rumbled Rawlegs.

'Steady up there,' calmed Moldoon, raising an arm. 'Ain't no call for raisin' bad tempers. I'm talkin' to the lady here, 'case yuh ain't noticed.'

'No, Mr Moldoon, I think we're all through.' Abigail tossed her hair again. 'The spread is not for sale, not now and at no time in the future. But I thank you for your interest. And now perhaps you will excuse Mr Rawlegs and myself. We have work to do.'

Moldoon hesitated a moment, the gaze darkening, the smoke curling thin and fragile from between his lips, before heeling the cheroot and slipping his hands to the pockets of his frock coat.

'Sorry to hear what yuh sayin', ma'am,' he smiled softly. 'Mebbe it's early days yet. Mebbe yuh'll change yuh mind.' The smile twisted cynically. 'In fact, I'm sure you will. I'll be around, rest assured.'

Trouble was, thought Rawlegs, when the men had finally mounted up and cleared the spread on the trail heading north, it was no idle threat: Moldoon would be around, for as long as it took, with whatever it took.

'I meant exactly what I said: the spread is not for sale and never will be,' Abigail had determined later that day, as she folded her arms dramatically and gazed over the dusk-shadowed reaches of the Washback. 'I trust I made that perfectly clear,' she had added, frowning. 'Did I?'

'Sure did, miss,' Rawlegs had assured. 'Leastways, yuh did to me. I ain't so certain about Moldoon.'

'You think he'll be back?' she had asked.

Oh, yes, he would be back, mused Rawlegs. He

would bide his time, but not for long; wait till he figured the moment for another call to be at its ripest for an easy picking. Then he would move.

'Well, he can pester all he likes,' Abigail had resolved. 'He won't get nowhere.'

How many times had he heard that?

'You just have to stand firm against types like Moldoon. That's so, isn't it Rawlegs? I am right, aren't I?'

Of course she was right. They had all been right, but that had never stopped Moldoon, had it?

Four

A whole week passed before Rawlegs was tempted to spit again in anger at the mention of Stove Moldoon. There had been no sight of him or his sidekicks at the homestead, nor, in the general hurly-burly of Abigail Grey taking over the spread and licking the ranch to her taste and liking, little time to dwell on the prospect of him. He was out of sight and therefore, by Abigail's reckoning, out of mind.

Not so to Rawlegs' thinking.

He had been only too ready to encourage the young woman in her endeavours and enthusiasm for home-making – it kept her mind clear of the loss of Sam Pooley and the circumstances of his dying – but he had always one eye turned to the trail and any place the shadows settled deepest.

First hint of a dust cloud heading his way, and Rawlegs was watching its progress like a hawk at a drifting prey; first movement in a shadow, and he had it spotted. You could never be too careful. One visit from Moldoon was never going to be the last.

But it was not until the morning he brought the buckboard into Resolute for fresh supplies and some lengths of new timber that he finally got to spitting.

'So you're ranch-handin' for Miss Grey, are yuh?' Sheriff Simmons had grinned. 'Lucky for you. Most fellas'd give an arm for a chance like that.' He had winked carefully from beneath the jaunty angle of the brim of his hat. 'Still, don't suppose yuh pose a threat on that score, eh, man of your age!'

'Save yuh breath on the smart remarks,' Rawlegs had growled. 'That the smartest yuh can do, I shouldn't bother. Best get to puttin' yuh energy where it matters, like trackin' down them scum murderers took out Sam. Lawman worth his badge would've gotten to it straight up.'

Mention of the shooting of Sam Pooley was guaranteed to rile the sheriff whatever his mood. 'Like I told yuh before 'til I'm sick of tellin' yuh, Blatch and them guns ridin' along of him are long gone; hundred miles, mebbe more. Cleared the territory weeks back.'

'Cleared it because yuh were a whole sight too slow gettin' to raise a posse. If you'd done that—'

'I ain't arguin' the matter no more,' Simmons had flared. 'You just get back to nurse-maidin' Miss Grey and watch yuh back for Stove Moldoon.'

'Moldoon? He in town?'

'Not himself, he ain't, but his boys've been askin' after yuh. T'ain't yuh health they're concerned about exactly, is it?'

It was then that Rawlegs had spat out his disgust and anger. 'Be too much to ask for yuh to keep an eye on 'em, I suppose? I mean, I guess yuh must be far too busy to get to doin' somethin' as ordinary as keepin' the town a decent, law-abidin' place!'

'Moldoon's men got every right to be here. Can't

run 'em out just 'cus yuh don't like their faces. They ain't done nothin' wrong.'

'Yet!' Rawlegs had spat again.

'Roll that wagon, old-timer,' Simmons had finally grinned, turning away. 'Get back to Miss Abigail's porch where it seems yuh belong.'

Rawlegs had still been muttering to himself even as he drove the buckboard clear of town and trundled to the trail to the Washback.

News of Moldoon's men lurking this close was no comfort and pointed clear enough to the land baron keeping his sights set tight on the Pooley spread. Did he figure on simply biding his time and playing a waiting game in the belief that the sheer demands of the ranch would inevitably prove too much for Abigail, that all he had to do was sit back, watch and reckon on her coming to him with an offer to sell?

How long was his patience? How deep his need? And just supposing the woman stuck to her belief in creating a home and a future for herself out there, what then? Would Moldoon finally shrug his shoulders and turn his back?

'Sure,' Rawlegs had mumbled to his thoughts, 'and hogs might get to sproutin' wings!'

He had reached the turn on the trail where it narrowed between a drift of rocks and boulders, known locally as The Elbows, his thoughts still buzzing and bubbling on the prospect of another visit to the ranch from Stove Moldoon, when the rider broke across the trail as if from nowhere.

'Whoa, damn yuh, whoa!' Rawlegs was already yelling, as the buckboard team veered first to the left, then right, left again, then, in a clamouring of hoofs, snorts and flying sweat, to a shuddering halt.

Rawlegs fell forward under the thrust of the momentum, heaved wildly on the reins, but held to his seat and glared defiantly at the bushy-browed, grinning rider facing him, the barrel of a Winchester probing over the sun glare.

One of Moldoon's sidekicks, soon to be joined from the cover of the rocks by his similarly grinning, gun-toting partners.

'We met before, ain't we, old-timer?' quipped bushy-brows.

'Don't need no remindin'. I can smell yuh!' croaked Rawlegs, spitting dirt and grit as he wiped the dust from his eyes.

'He really is a lippy sonofabitch, ain't he?' hummed the younger man. 'Somebody should do somethin' about that lip.' His gaze darkened.

'Yuh gettin' ambitious, ain't yuh, boy?' croaked Rawlegs again.

'See what I mean – real lippy.'

'Ease it up,' sniffed the bony-faced third man, lowering the barrel of his rifle.

'We got a message for the lady back there,' said bushy-brows, shifting to the roll of his mount. 'From Moldoon.'

'So why ain't yuh deliverin' it personal?' asked Rawlegs. 'Yuh gettin' petticoat-spooked or somethin'?' He spat deliberately between the riders and pushed the brim of his hat clear of his eyes.

'You just tell the lady as how she's got a week – one whole week, seven full days – before Mr Moldoon comes callin' again. Yuh got that?' scowled bushy-brows.

'I got it.' Rawlegs flexed his grip on the leather.

'I'll have Miss Grey bake him a cake!'

'Just cut the quippin', old-timer. We ain't in the mood for it.'

'That we surely ain't,' sneered the younger man. 'Not one bit. What say we teach old lippy here a lesson in manners? Shut that mouth of his for a while.'

'I'm for that,' grinned bony-face. 'Beginnin' right here.' He nudged his mount to the side of the buckboard, reached into it, grabbed at the supplies and tipped a half sack of flour to the trail.

'What the hell—' spluttered Rawlegs, only to have his protests drowned in the mocking laughter of the men.

Bushy-brows had tugged at another sack, hoisted it from the wagon and hurled its contents across the dirt.

'Hey, now, look at this, will yuh?' whistled the younger man, heaving a roll of dress fabric across his saddle. 'What yuh reckon, fellas – bet the pretty woman back there'd look good in this, eh? Yessir! Real sassy charmer!'

'Yuh just put that right back, yuh hear?' blustered Rawlegs, almost losing his balance as he reached for the fabric.

The man tossed the roll into the scrub, angled his Winchester on it and shot it through till it was riddled with holes.

The sidekicks whooped and jeered and shouted, ranging their mounts round the wagon, grabbing at whatever they could reach and drag to the trail and either scuffing with dirt, shooting to pieces, emptying or destroying, including the lengths of timber under the pounding hoofs of the mounts.

'Know somethin'?' yelled bony-face above the rabble, snorts and Rawlegs' spitting curses, 'I don't figure for the fella needin' this old buckboard. Past its best, ain't it, and them horses there sure look as if they could use a spot of freedom? Hell, wouldn't be much of loss to woman of property likes of Abigail Grey, would it?'

'That's my man!' yelled bushy-brows.

'Get to it! And you, old-timer, get yourself down from there,' jeered the younger man. 'I got a notion to settle that lippy mouth of yours.'

Bony-face was pulling at the tack, the horses snorting, sweating, stamping, Rawlegs already stumbling in the swirling dirt under a hail of slaps, taunts and threats, and bushy-brows readying the tip of a glowing cigar for the flame that would engulf the wagon, when the three fast shots ripped out of the boulders like the blaze of dragons' tongues.

The first spun the cigar from bushy-brows' fingers, leaving a surge of blood bubbling across his hand, a cursed cry of pain hissing from his lips, and a blackened bewildered scowl creasing his face as he grabbed at loose reins for his balance.

The second whirled bony-face's hat from his head, crashing the sidekick flat in his saddle, his eyes round and white as washed plates.

But it was the third, in its vicious blaze and screaming whine, that widened Rawlegs' gaze as he watched the jeering younger man's head thrown back, eyes rolling, his mouth open on a sound that might have been the splitting of rock, and the deep red stain at his shoulder spread like a flood until it seemed his shirt was sodden.

'Sonofa-goddamn-bitch!' groaned bushy-brows,

wheeling his prancing mount through a full circle.

'Pull clear!' yelled bony-face. 'Get the hell out. Fella's holed-up there in them rocks.'

The younger man had slumped forward across his mount's neck, but miraculously stayed in the saddle under the sudden tugging of reins as bony-face dragged horse and rider from the wagon and on to the main trail.

A fourth shot, a fifth, sixth, ten in all, snarled at the dirt of the pounding hoofs, scattering sand, swirling dust, lifting small rocks as Moldoon's men whipped their mounts to a frenzy and headed for Resolute.

It was a full minute before Rawlegs had managed to spit the dirt from his mouth, blinked it from his eyes, squirmed at the grating prickle of it in the sweat that lathered his back, rubbed it from the stubble at his chin and staggered to the buckboard team to calm them.

'Whoa now. Easy there. Easy. . . . Easy . . .' he comforted, his eyes still blinking on the swirling dirt. He narrowed his blurred, watery gaze on the sweep of rocks and boulders. 'Just where in hell did them shots. . . ?'

And then he saw him, the tall, tanned, well-mannered stranger he had stood with in the street on the day of Sam's funeral. 'Well, I'll be darned,' he muttered, noting the familiar set of the fellow's hat against the glare, the Winchester cradled across his body, the watchful, piercing gleam in his eyes.

'Howdy,' said the man quietly. 'We meet again.'

Five

'Don't go a deal on the company yuh keep,' called the man, swinging his gaze to the disappearing dust cloud on the trail into town. 'Yuh could do without 'em, I reckon.'

'Say that again,' groaned Rawlegs, removing his hat to mop a bandanna over his bald pate. 'Real grateful to yuh there, mister, yuh happenin' along and showin' them Moldoon scum ... where'd yuh learn to shoot like that, f'Cris'sake? Hell, I ain't seen faster shootin' from a Winchester since Clay Willetts took out the Spencer brothers back in forty-eight, and that weren't nothin' special 'side of what yuh just did. . . . We ain't been formally introduced, have we? Name's Rawstone, but everybody hereabouts calls me Rawlegs. Pleased to meet yuh, mister.'

Rawlegs smiled generously, settled his hat and stepped forward, his hand reaching out for the stranger's.

'McAdams,' said the man, joining his hand to the shake. 'Heard of you way back,' he added carefully.

'Yuh did?' gulped Rawlegs, slapping his lips. 'Well, ain't that somethin'? Can't figure how, though, seein' as how I ain't set foot off the Washback in twenty

31

years, not since the Runnin' Wolf uprisin' and
massacre back at Tooney's Drift, and then only. . . .
Why, yuh'd be no more than a nipper back then.'

'We got a mutual friend,' said the man. '*Had* a
mutual friend.'

'We did?' frowned Rawlegs. 'How come? Who was
he?'

'Sam Pooley.'

'Captain Pooley? But how'd—'

'I served along of him with the Twenty-third 'til
we both took the payout to retirement. I was his
number two – Lieutenant McAdams.'

'Well, now, ain't that just somethin' to bring the
sun out on a black day? I'll be darned, damned if I
won't! You and the captain. . . . My, my, would yuh
believe it? And now, here yuh are and. . . .'

The old man gulped again and stared hard and
unblinking into McAdams's eyes. 'Heck, what the hell
am I sayin' here? Yuh were right there in the street
. . . saw the coffin . . . the mourners, Miss Abigail. . . .
Heard me goin' on about them gunslingers. And yuh
never said, did yuh? Not a word. Hell, yuh must've
thought—'

'Sam wrote me,' said McAdams, patting the breast
pocket of his shirt. 'A long letter. Longest I ever had.
Promised he would day we split trails out Wyomin'
way.' He paused a moment. 'Told me a whole lot
about the way of things out here.'

Rawlegs blinked and tightened the stare. 'He did?
What sort of things?'

'About the spread here, all that land; about Miss
Abigail and yourself, the town, its folk. Said as how
he planned to wed and asked if I'd stand as his best
man. Oh, yes, he sure had plenty to tell me.'

McAdams paused again. 'Specially about Stove Moldoon,' he added slowly, the gaze sharpening from the shade beneath the brim of his hat. 'A whole lot about him.'

Rawlegs swallowed and wiped the sweat from his brow. 'That why yuh here?' he asked drily. 'Because of Moldoon?'

'He's one of the reasons.'

'But Captain Pooley couldn't have known then about Blatch—'

McAdams shouldered the Winchester. 'Time we cleared up the mess here, got that team into shade and watered up. I'll give yuh a hand.'

'Sure, sure,' said Rawlegs, turning to the scattered supplies. 'Not that there's a deal here worth savin', damn it! When I think—'

'Let's do it. We'll talk later.'

'You bet,' grinned Rawlegs. 'Don't figure on them lick-spittin' scumbags showin' their faces again.'

'Pity,' grunted McAdams, stepping to the buckboard.

Sounded as if he meant it, too, mused Rawlegs.

'But will he? I mean why should he? He's got a life. Maybe he's got plans for living it some place else.' Abigail folded her arms against the chill night air and walked slowly into the shadows at the far end of the homestead veranda. 'Why would he want to stay here? You'd feel the same, wouldn't you?' she added, turning to stare at Rawlegs.

The old man examined the glowing bowl of his pipe and relaxed to the slow momentum and creak of the cane rocker. 'I might,' he said with an almost off-handed sigh. 'But I might not. It would depend.'

'On what?'

'On precisely what my friend had taken the trouble to write to me about at such length. Just that, Miss Abi, just that.'

'But we can't ask him, can we?' said Abigail. 'We couldn't do that. It's none of our business. Sam's letter is private.'

'Can't ask, but we can sure as hell make a guess, can't we? Ain't no harm in that. And I got a pretty good idea of what the captain put pen to paper over. Yessir, a good idea.' Rawlegs rocked pointedly for a moment. 'Yuh want for me to tell yuh?' he blinked.

' 'Course I do,' said Abigail.

The rocker creaked again, then fell silent. 'Way I see it,' began Rawlegs, 'the captain had come to some fair notion of Stove Moldoon's interest in the spread here, and knowin' Moldoon's ways of doin' business he'd have seen straight up that one man standin' alone weren't goin' to be a deal of use, 'specially when the sheriff here ain't worth a strangled spit – beggin' yuh pardon, miss. Fella of the likes of McAdams – and I've seen him handlin' that Winchester remember – would be worth a dozen of Moldoon's guns. And,' winked Rawlegs, 'he'd have his best man right on hand come the big day, wouldn't he?'

Abigail bit at her lip and tightened the fold of her arms. 'So, Mr McAdams begins the long journey from Wyoming, but meantime—'

'Meantime we know what happened here, don't we? We do that. . . . Time McAdams hits Resolute, his good friend Sam Pooley is on his way to Boot Hill. Harsh fact, Miss Abi, but true. Ain't no sayin' other.'

Abigail turned to stare into the night. 'Even so, he left town,' she murmured, 'and then came back. Where did he go, and why did he come back?' She turned to Rawlegs again. 'Can you answer me that?'

'Mebbe I can too,' said Rawlegs, setting the rocker into creaking motion. 'Two fleas to a bad smell, he's been out the Washback, and where out the Washback? I'll tell yuh—'

'No, I'll tell you.'

The voice snapped out of the darkness like the crack of old bone as the man came to the edge of the pale lantern glow, halted and let his piercing gaze glide across the veranda.

Abigail caught her breath and put a hand to her mouth. The cane rocker creaked. Rawlegs' pipe flared in a sudden cloud of smoke.

'Sorry if I took yuh by surprise,' said McAdams. 'Just lookin' to my mount there at the stablin'. Couldn't help overhearin' your conversation.'

'Damnit, fella, why don't yuh step up here and say what's on yuh mind?' Rawlegs rocked noisily, blew smoke and stared long and hard. 'I'm right, aren't I? Yuh been out the Washback. Yuh been scoutin' out Moldoon. Right?'

McAdams shifted his weight and glanced quickly at Abigail. 'S'right,' he said. 'That letter Sam wrote me told of how Moldoon had been frettin' at Sam over his spread for some time. Moldoon's buildin' himself an empire – and by any means.'

'Yuh can say that again,' grunted Rawlegs. 'Been doin' it these past fifteen years, and gettin' greedier the more he swallows.' The old man removed the pipe from his mouth, spat clear to the dirt, and grunted again. 'Sorry, Miss Abi. Way I'm feelin' right now it's all enough to make a fella spit.'

'Bigger Moldoon's holdin' and cattle herd gets, the more he needs,' McAdams went on. 'Specially when it comes to water for the cattle.'

'The Old Yellow,' murmured Abigail vaguely. 'He wants the land flanking the river.'

'That's right, miss. All the spread yuh got east to the water and as far as yuh go to Eagle Springs where he figures for there bein' a rail-head once the line comes through from the west. He'll be shippin' enough beef off the Washback to feed the nation – and at his price.'

Rawlegs creaked the rocker to and fro. 'Yeah, well,' he grinned, puffing extravagantly on the pipe, 'he's gotta get the land first, ain't he? This land, mister. And we ain't for sellin'! That so, Miss Abi?'

'I have no plans—' began Abigail, but cut herself short as McAdams stepped closer to the veranda.

'No disrespect, miss, but t'ain't a question of your plannin',' he said sharply. 'I seen what Moldoon's got back there on his spread: enough guns to found an army, and enough money to keep supplyin' it with all it needs for as long as it takes.'

'What are you saying, Mr McAdams?' asked Abigail, hugging herself against a sudden shiver.

'If you ain't for sellin', miss – and I can see yuh ain't – then Moldoon'll be all for threatenin' and terrorizin' yuh 'til yuh mebbe only too grateful to be clear of the spread. I know, I seen his type at work before.'

Abigail shivered again. 'So what do we do?'

'Do? I'll tell yuh what we do,' spat Rawlegs through a billow of pipe smoke. 'We get ourselves organized. Get our own guns—'

'Start a war across the Washback?' snapped McAdams. 'Lose yuh spread and mebbe get yourselves killed into the bargain? Don't look to be much of a prospect from where I'm standin'.'

'So,' spat Rawlegs again, rocking wildly, 'what you suggestin', mister? Yuh figured on some plan?'

'You're very welcome to stay, Mr McAdams. You know that,' added Abigail hurriedly. 'Not that I'm suggesting you should simply because—'

'I'm here for my good friend, Sam Pooley, miss. Wouldn't have it no other way. I owe Captain Pooley more times than I care to recall. Least I can do now is. . . . Yeah, well, least I can do now is make certain the woman he entrusted with his property ain't robbed of it. So, yes, I have a plan, if you can call it that. T'ain't much, and there's only the three of us, but mebbe that's all we need.'

Hardly needed a hand back there on the trail, did you, pondered Rawlegs, easing his body to the rocker's slow creaks. Scattered Moldoon's rats faster than a rattler in a hen coop. So maybe the fellow does have a plan, he mused.

The old man settled to the rocker's comfort, conscious for the first time that night of the chill breeze blowing off the Washback from the east.

Mite early for a wind that mean to be getting up this time of the year, he thought.

Six

A handful of miles away on that same night as the chill east wind whipped off the bleak emptiness of the Washback, the lights burned late in Resolute's only bar.

The three men seated at the table in the corner had shown not the slightest inclination of calling it a day and heading for their beds. They had eaten early, dismissed the attentions of the bar girls in favour of a bottle of best whiskey, and lapsed into a deep and concentrated debate among themselves.

They were still debating, still drinking, when Joe Heane, the saloon proprietor, lowered the lantern glows to a mere flicker and resigned himself to a long night. He would remain in the bar for as long as the men stayed talking and drinking.

That had been the deal struck on the day Moldoon's men had checked in.

And they were not the types for arguing with, and certainly not on this night. . . .

'Well,' growled bushy-brows behind a rumbling belch, 'yuh still of the same mind? Yuh still goin' to wait, or yuh goin' to get some sense through that split-pea yuh got for a brain? Choice is yours.'

'Damnit,' moaned bony-face, rolling his eyes, 'I ain't sure. One minute I'm with yuh, the next – ar, I don't know. Hell, what'll Stove say if we get to goin' our own ways? He hands out the orders and we follow 'em. Always been the same.'

'Yeah, well, Moldoon ain't here, is he, and won't be for days,' said bushy-brows, wincing as he rested his bandaged hand on the table. 'Meantime, we got some stingy-eyed shootist totin' a Winchester out there, and two-bits to a whore's purse he's workin' for the Grey woman. So I say we do the sensible thing and take him out before he gets to settlin' his butt. First light. No messin'. Fast shootin' and gone. Won't know what hit him. What yuh say? Yuh with us, or ain't yuh?'

' 'Course he's with us,' moaned the younger man, laying a hand to his wounded shoulder. 'When ain't he been? 'Sides, he owes me, so he can do my shootin' for me, seein' as I'm a mite inconvenienced here.'

'Well . . .' drawled bony-face.

'Quit stallin', f'Cris'sake. Anybody'd think we were plannin' on shootin' the state governor! Only a fella, ain't he? Handy with a rifle, for sure, but he got a deal lucky back there, didn't he? Took us all by surprise. Weren't figurin' for him, were we?'

'Supposin' we figure it wrong next time?' frowned bony-face.

'Supposin' we don't?' grinned bushy-brows. 'Supposin' we take the fella out, now ain't that goin' to spook that woman somewhat? Ain't that goin' to put the shivers through her, and ain't Mr Moldoon goin' to be one heap grateful to us? Bet yuh ain't thought of that, have yuh?'

'No, can't say I have, and yuh could be right.'

' 'Course I'm right.'

' 'Course he is,' said the younger man replenishing the glasses. 'Let's drink to it, eh?'

'Hold on,' urged bony-face. 'How we goin' to do it exactly?'

'Straightforward, nothin' fancy,' said bushy-brows. 'Sun-up we hit the spread. Real soft, real quiet. Know the place well enough, don't we? Took a good look round day we were there with Moldoon. Certain as night the Winchester man'll be sleepin' in the bunkhouse, mebbe that old man along of him. Mebbe we'll take 'em both out, eh? How about that? Miss-flouncy-butt-Grey ain't goin' to be so flouncy cartin' a couple more bodies to Boot Hill, is she? Be all for sellin' up fast as she can. And ain't that goin' to settle real sweet with Moldoon? I'll say!'

'See,' said the younger man, 'more yuh think about it, better it gets, don't it?'

'But what if—' began bony-face.

'No "what-ifs", no more thinkin' on it. We do it. Sun-up. And now, we drink to it. Right? Good. Somebody go wake that dozin' barman there.'

The cold, whining draught whipping under the door to Sheriff Bart Simmons's office was just another annoyance adding to the misery of his long night.

East wind cutting clear off the Washback at this time of the year, he pondered, easing to the warmth of the stove at the back of the office? Hell, never been known. World was going mad.

He spread his hands to the hotplate and rubbed them together, his thoughts beginning to spin and spiral again. Damn it, he was going to have to do something, make a move, any move, before it all got

out of hand. Just no saying, was there, what
Moldoon's men might get to next?

But maybe a whole sight more worrying was just
who it was had tangled with them. Some hot-shot
stranger with a Winchester siding along of Rawlegs,
they had said, still nursing their wounds and shattered pride on their return to town that afternoon.
Yet he had seen the old man load his wagon at the
mercantile, spoken to him, watched him head out for
the trail, all very much on his own up there on the
buckboard.

So where had he met the stranger, where had the
man come from; why had he got to a fight with
Moldoon's men, and, more important, where was the
stranger now?

Could he be in town? Unlikely. Somebody would
have said. Out the Washback? Not in this wind. Still
with Rawlegs; maybe bunking down at the Pooley
spread? Possibly – in fact, very probably.

Maybe he should go take a look for himself, he
mused, crossing the office to the dark window and
peering through it to the night street beyond. Light
still burning at the saloon, he noted. Moldoon's men
licking their wounds.

He would roust a couple of deputies, ride out to
the Pooley spread at sun-up, see just who it was had
the guts, the skill and good enough reason to cross
three of Stove Moldoon's picked gunslingers and
send them scuttling back down the trail, tails tight
between legs.

Meantime, do something about that draught.

Rawlegs had spent the better part of that night
listening to the wind whip itself to its mischievous

worst through the bunkhouse. Slightest gap, and it was there, setting to a creaking groan anything hanging loose, not nailed tight, twisting on a rusty hook, swinging on a worn rope, until, when he closed his eyes, it seemed as if the whole Washback world was on the move, or trying to be.

But there was more to his restless tossing beneath the blankets than a change in the weather through the eastern hills.

There was McAdams, the sound of his voice, the hour he had spent talking in the soft glow of the veranda lantern, telling of his first meeting with Captain Sam Pooley, the instant rapport and understanding between them, the skirmishes, close shaves and prairie wars they had shared as fellow officers and comrades, their last days together out there on the Wyoming trails, the final parting, the unspoken certainty they would meet again, somewhere, sometime.

'But I never figured for standin' in a street watchin' him carted to a hole on Boot Hill,' he had concluded, his stare fixed like a light on Abigail's wet gaze.

And now, Rawlegs had sighed to himself more than once through the night, McAdams was here, with not a deal of a plan to trim the greed of Stove Moldoon, but enough hatred and bitterness against the miserable end that had befallen his friend to maybe prove one hell of a burr in the fellow's boot.

Sure he would, Rawlegs had thought, just a pity he had not been around to reckon with Blatch and his sidekicks.

'Fact of it is, Miss Abigail,' McAdams had said, his gaze back from the past, steady and gentler, 'Sam

Pooley left yuh this spread. He wanted yuh to build the rest of your life here. Seems a fine enough notion to me, and so yuh shall. . . .'

You bet, Rawlegs had thought; fine words, fine principle, and no question the fellow was needed. But the real fact of it was that Stove Moldoon had never been much for the finer points and principles of anything, least of all other folk and however the law stood to them.

And like the man had said, there was only the three of them.

Somewhere between his thoughts of finer points and principles and the first hint of the morning light across the Washback, Rawlegs drifted into a deep sleep.

And he might have stayed there, tight in the blanket, with the morning already calmer and quieter, had it not been for the creak and grating whine of the bunkhouse door where it swung to the lighter wind.

'Hell,' he cursed, struggling upright, blinking, as his stockinged feet slid to the floor, 'some folk use a door like it weren't there!'

And was still cursing McAdams for rising so darned early, when he realized through another blurred blink, that the fellow's bunk was empty and, from the touch of it, had been for some time.

He grunted, scratched his bald pate, rubbed his stubble, and gazed at the open door still swinging on the wind. Had McAdams simply opted for an early start, taken a stroll, maybe gone for fresh water. . . . Who was he kidding? Fellow's Winchester had gone.

So maybe something had disturbed him.

An early visitor.

An unwelcome early visitor.

Rawlegs dressed quickly, silently, to his shirt, pants, boots, settled his hat, brim turned back, and edged to the side of the open door, his eyes narrowed on the space and the shadowy emptiness of the homestead paddock.

All quiet. No lights at the house. Soft curl of smoke from the stack. Corralled horses resting easy. Shadows looked to be empty.

But not all of them.

Something moving out there, side of the hay-barn, between it and the sprawl of stabling. Shape of a figure, no doubt about that. But not McAdams. Too squat, too slim.

'Damn it, Moldoon's men!' hissed Rawlegs, squinting for a closer look. Hell, if any one of them managed to get to Miss Abi, if she was still sleeping. . . .

The old man slid from the bunkhouse, latched the door closed behind him and was looking round wildly for where to head for the slimmest cover, when the first shot rang out across the half-light, the heaped night shadows, like a scream, the blaze of it spitting in a flash of flame.

Rawlegs fell back against the bunkhouse door, his gaze in a flurry of blinking as he watched McAdams move across the paddock, the Winchester ripping its lead first at the figure at the hay-barn, then at a man following in his steps. Both were flung to the ground in an instant, the bodies twisted and unmoving.

A third man, racing across the dirt for the far end of the corral, faltered in a scramble of steps, halted, breathless, one hand clutching his bandaged shoulder, the other fumbling uselessly for a holstered Colt.

McAdams raised the Winchester, waited, the aim steady, as if baiting the man to draw, fired a single shot that kicked dirt at the fellow's heels, then lowered the barrel as the man raced on to his hitched mount.

He was letting the sidekick ride out, thought Rawlegs on a long, dry swallow, back to Stove Moldoon!

Lights blazed in the homestead. Horses snorted and whinnied, some bucking in a blind panic along the corral fencing.

Hoofs pounded from somewhere back of the bunkhouse. Riders coming in. Men shouting, dirt flying, blood spreading and staining.

War had been declared!

And the sun was not yet up.

Seven

'Yuh drop that rifle real easy, mister, and yuh stand back where I can see yuh. Easy, yuh hear? And right now!' Sheriff Simmons barked his orders from the saddle of his mount, a Colt gleaming stiff and levelled in his hand, two deputies, guns similarly levelled, flanking him.

'Now hold on there some, Bart Simmons,' began Rawlegs, moving clear of the bunkhouse. 'I been here all along. I seen exactly what happened.'

'So did I,' snapped Simmons, his stare flat as wet rock on McAdams as the man dropped the Winchester, stepped back a pace and half raised his arms in surrender. 'Better,' mouthed the sheriff.

'Them scumbags of Moldoon's crept in here—' began Rawlegs again.

'I seen 'em. I ain't blind,' said Simmons, circling his mount round McAdams. 'Didn't look to be doin' no harm to me. Didn't see 'em shootin' back none.'

'No harm, f'Cris'sake!' hissed Rawlegs. 'Mister, I'm tellin' yuh them rats were all steamed up to kill McAdams there and mebbe m'self into the bargain. Lord above knows what they had planned for Miss Abigail.'

'McAdams, eh?' grinned Simmons. 'So that's yuh name.'

'Real good friend of Sam Pooley's,' nodded Rawlegs. 'Him and Captain Pooley—'

'All right, Rawlegs, yuh leave it right there for now,' said McAdams, shifting his gaze to the cold-eyed deputies resting easy on slack reins.

'Damnit, man, somebody's gotta speak up here,' flared Rawlegs, thrusting himself across the dirt to face the sheriff square on. 'Let's get this straight, once and for all. And yuh ain't threatenin' me none, Bart Simmons, with that spit-licked Colt, no more yuh are with button-booted sidekicks. So yuh listen up some. Right?

'Them gunslingers in Moldoon's pay – pair of 'em makin' worm meat there, and good riddance too – bushwhacked me and my outfit down the town trail yesterday. S'right. Bushwhacked me. And they would sure as hell have finished me if it had not been for McAdams gettin' among 'em. Yuh got that, have yuh? Hearin' me clear? Right. So it ain't no earth-shatterin' surprise, is it, to figure as how them thick-skulled sidekicks would come scurryin' back sooner or later with the notion of levellin' the score? Yuh got that? Still followin' me? Right. So they did, didn't they, first crack of light this mornin'. I know, I seen 'em – and so did McAdams here, thank the Lord.'

Rawlegs slapped his lips, spat across the dirt, and pushed back the brim of his hat. 'It hadn't been for McAdams bein' awake, him and me'd been murdered in our bunks. No question of it. So yuh'd best be thankin' my friend here for riddin' the territory of a vermin—'

'I'm takin' him in,' announced Simmons.

'You're what?'

'Yuh heard. I'm takin' him in.'

'On what charge, f'Cris'sake?'

'Murder. Cold-blooded as it comes.'

'But that ain't—'

'*Gentlemen – for Heaven's sake, is there no sanity here?*'

Abigail Grey's voice cracked across the chill morning air like the sudden snap of sheet ice.

'Hey, now, miss—' muttered Rawlegs.

McAdams swung round to face her, his gaze glinting.

The deputies stiffened and leaned back from the necks of their mounts. Sheriff Simmons put a hand to the brim of his hat, and smiled. 'Mornin', miss,' he said quietly. 'Sorry to be disturbin' yuh this time of day.'

'Disturbin', f'Cris'sake!' groaned Rawlegs.

'And what precisely is going on here?' asked Abigail fighting the tremor of a shiver. 'Hasn't there been enough—?' The shiver took a grip.

Rawlegs bustled to the woman's side.

'Like I say, miss,' continued Simmons, 'sorry to be disturbin' yuh, but it's all through now. I'll have them bodies there moved soon as I can, and meantime I'm takin' this fella, McAdams, here into town. He'll be spendin' a while behind bars waitin' on circuit Judge Makepiece's next visit.'

McAdams stayed silent, unmoving. Rawlegs groaned and ran a hand across his eyes. The deputies grinned. Simmons simply stared.

'Is that wise, Mr Simmons?' asked Abigail, with a disarming air of innocence. 'I mean, I knew these

men . . . those lyin' out there, the one that rode out
. . they were here. They're Moldoon's men. And I
can assure you, Sheriff, they were not at all
friendly. The very opposite, in fact. They were quite
intimidating, so I am not one bit surprised to
hear—'

'That may be so, miss,' said Simmons hurriedly,
his gaze narrowing on McAdams. 'And I ain't
doubtin' what yuh tellin' me; no more am I doubtin'
as how Moldoon's men got a mite over zealous with
Rawlegs—'

'Over zealous, my butt!' cursed the old man.
'Beggin' yuh pardon, Miss Abi.'

'But that don't change nothin' of what's happened
here this mornin',' bristled Simmons. 'This is a
straight up, no-holds shootin', miss, and yuh can't
say other. McAdams comes to town, and I'd be
obliged if yuh'd let me get to my duty.'

'Duty! Bah! Hog-swill!' growled Rawlegs, spitting
fiercely through the scuffed dirt. 'Didn't hear yuh
boastin' to no duty when they shot Sam Pooley.
Didn't see yuh draggin' yuh pup-nosed deputies
along of yuh when yuh could've been ridin' to bring
in that sonofabitch, Blatch, did I? Nossir! Sure as
hell didn't see no *duty* then!'

'Leave it,' snapped McAdams, lowering his arms
to his sides. 'This the way the sheriff here wants it,
this is how it'll be. For now.'

Simmons's gaze narrowed until the slits were
tight as black scratches. 'Let's move,' he drawled. 'Go
get the man's horse and let's get out of here.' He
tipped the brim of his hat again to Abigail Grey. 'I'll
bid yuh good mornin', miss.'

'See yuh in Hell first,' grated Rawlegs beneath his

breath, adding a stab of spittle on the back of the curse.

McAdams walked ahead to the corral without another word.

'Plain as the nose on yuh face, miss – plain as the nose on *my* face more like! – that two-bit sheriff is usin' McAdams as a pawn against playin' Moldoon's game. Judge Makepiece ain't due in Resolute this side of Fall. No, all Simmons wants to do is hand McAdams to Moldoon's rats and take the credit and pay-off for his effort. Hog-swill!'

Rawlegs stomped along the line of the corral fencing, scuffing the dirt and mopping his bald head with an already sodden bandanna as he went. He reached the end of the line, pocketed the bandanna and thrust his hat on his head. 'We're goin' to have to do somethin', miss,' he said, his stare level and fixed on Abigail Grey where she leaned on the fence, nuzzling the nose of a young horse. 'And we're goin' to have to do it before the sidekick that got clear reaches Moldoon with his story and the whole rotten empire gets to thrashin' at our butts.'

'Mr McAdams let the sidekick go, didn't he?' said the woman.

'Sure. He wanted to bring Moldoon here, to our territory, on our terms but that didn't include him bein' behind bars, damn it!'

'So we need Mr McAdams out of jail. And soon.'

Rawlegs sighed. 'Yes, miss. Just like that.' He coughed lightly. 'Any ideas?'

'Only one,' smiled Abigail, patting the horse's head as she pushed herself clear of the fencing. 'Might work; might not. Shall we try?'

'Tell me,' croaked Rawlegs, clearing his throat. 'I'm listenin' real good!'

Eight

'Your pa'd skin the hide off me for goin' along with this – and I ain't foolin'.' Rawlegs winced on the jolt of the buckboard, gripped the reins and fixed his gaze on the trail ahead.

'But pa isn't here,' said Abigail, bracing herself at the old man's side. 'So he's never going to know.'

'Don't you bet on it,' huffed Rawlegs. He smacked his lips noisily. 'Probably watchin' the pair of us right now. Lookin' down from somewheres up there. . . . Hell, miss, do we have to do it this way? There's gotta be somethin' else.'

'Name it.'

Rawlegs buried a sigh in his throaty groan. 'Well,' he began, wincing again, 'suppose we just wait on Moldoon gettin' here. Supposin' we do some sorta deal with him.'

'Nobody gets to honest dealing with Stove Moldoon. Said so yourself.'

'True, but, then . . . there's gotta be a first time.'

Abigail brushed a smear of dust from her dress and tightened the silk scarf at her neck. 'You don't believe that, Rawlegs, and you know full well you don't. Just saying it. No, we try this my way, a touch of feminine wiles, and if that doesn't work—'

'It's if it does that worries me, damn it! Hell, miss, you got any notion at all of what yuh might be lettin' yourself in for? Yuh given a thought to where it might end?'

'Some,' said Abigail, her expression set stubbornly unmoving. 'Not too much. I could go off the whole idea. But if you do your part, we might, just might, pull it off.' She brushed at another smear of dust. 'Anyway, it's all we've got.'

'Yuh could mebbe think again about the spread.'

'The spread is not for bargaining. Never was. Now, do you know exactly what to do once we hit town?'

Rawlegs flicked the reins and breathed deeply. 'After I've fixed it with Barney at the livery – and he'll be with us, you bet – I wait 'til I seen yuh make contact with Simmons. I watch for you and him crossin' to the saloon—'

'Stayin' out of sight while you're doing it.'

'Like yuh say, miss. Then, just before yuh pass through the batwings you'll give me a signal with that scarf you're wearin'.'

Abigail fingered the folds of it. 'If it stays at my neck it means there's more than one deputy still at the jail. If I remove it, you will know there's only one. And if there's only one—'

'Yuh leave it to me from there on. I know what to do. What concerns me a whole lot more is you bein' with Simmons, and I gotta say it, Miss Abi, I wouldn't trust that scumbag hidin' behind a badge any more than I would . . . than I would, well, I'd best not say it, not in front of a lady. Damn it, yuh seen it yourself only this mornin': dirty dealin'. All I'm sayin' is—'

'I know what you're saying Rawlegs, and I'm hearing you. Don't doubt it for a moment.' She placed a hand on his arm and smiled softly. 'Trust me. I can take care of myself. Just remember, if this has a half a chance of working, we have to see it through. We shan't get a second shot at it. And nor will Mr McAdams.'

Rawlegs snapped the reins and swallowed. Town coming up there, quiet as a whisper. Pray it stays that way, he thought.

But who was he kidding?

'One axe-handle is pretty much like another, Rawlegs. All the same price. Fingerin' 'em don't make 'em any cheaper.' Miras Coutts rubbed his hands through his storekeeper's apron and glared over the rims of his spindly spectacles. 'Yuh buyin' or just passin' the time? Been standin' there twenty minutes.'

Rawlegs drew his hand quickly from the display of handles, shrugged and grinned lamely. 'Clean got to day-dreamin' there, Miras,' he said, thrusting his hands to his trouser pockets.

'Don't have the time for it m'self,' grunted the storekeeper, busying himself among his goods. 'Got a business to run here, 'case yuh ain't noticed. No time for starin'.'

'Seen anythin' of Simmons today?' ventured Rawlegs.

'Not since early on. Brought in a prisoner. Stranger off the Washback. Got to tanglin' with them fellas ridin' for Moldoon. They *say* – some town folk, that is – stranger was out on the old Pooley spread. Miss Grey's place. Yuh see anythin' of him? Bet yuh did at that, eh?'

'Mebbe I did,' murmured Rawlegs, returning his gaze to the street beyond the store window.

He waited a moment before letting it settle on the door to the sheriff's office. Hell, just what was going on behind it?

'Well?' said Coutts irritably. 'Yuh buyin' or ain't yuh? Can't stand here tradin' gossip.'

'Know your trouble, Miras?' smiled Rawlegs, selecting a handle and smoothing it through his fingers. 'Yuh don't give a fella no time for browsin'. Now, somebody comes lookin' for a horse, I ain't goin' to go rushin' him into buyin', am I? Give him time. Let him chew round it a while.' His glance flicked back to the sheriff's office. Door was still closed. 'And, who knows, when the time does come—'

'What in tarnation yuh on about there? That's an axe-handle yuh fingerin'; t'ain't no high pedigree stallion!'

'No, that it most certainly ain't. . . .' Shape there at the office window. Might be Simmons. 'But on the other hand, principle of purchase still applies, don't it?'

'Principle of purchase – and what in hell's name, is that? I ain't never heard of no such thing.'

'Exactly. And that's the trouble. . . .' Shape has left the window. Where is Simmons? Where is Miss Abi? What is happening back there? 'If you'd given a fella the proper time to browse, why, there ain't no sayin' as to how many handles he might have bought. . . .'

Sheriff's door was open. Miss Abigail stepping to the boardwalk, Simmons right behind her.

'I'll mebbe take this one,' snapped Rawlegs, drop-ping the handle and selecting another all in one movement. 'Thanks, Miras. Pay yuh next time I'm in town, eh? Gotta rush right now.'

'Clean out of his mind,' murmured the store-keeper, watching Rawlegs sidle away to the street shadows, the axe-handle hanging loose in his grip. 'Age finally gettin' to him. Shame.'

If your pa could see you now. . . . Rawlegs blinked as he backed deeper into the shadowed alley between the store and Charlie Winns' saddlery, his gaze fixed on Sheriff Simmons and a smiling, laughing Abigail Grey strolling provocatively at his side.

Hell, he thought, squinting in his concentration, his shoulders squirming against the sweat across his back, she had pulled it off, just like she said she would, got that no-hoper, double-dealing lawman eating out of her hand.

He gulped. Easy – but now what? He would wait for the signal, act on it accordingly, and after that Miss Abi would be on her own. Hell!

He shifted a step to the left. They were still cross-ing the street, Simmons shepherding Miss Abigail as if putting a hand to porcelain, a soft, lecherous grin at his lips. Sonofabitch!

They had paused now front of the steps to the saloon boardwalk, Abigail laughing coyly, almost shyly – until you spotted the gleam in her eye! Rawlegs grunted. Easy enough to read Simmons' mind. . . .

Hold it, they were moving on, up the steps, on to the boardwalk, to the batwings. Another pause. Miss

Abi was fingering the scarf, drawing it slowly from her neck.

That was it! The signal! Now he knew what to do.

Rawlegs slumped back against the clapboard wall, wiped the sweat from his face, blinked again and swallowed. His grip tightened on the axe-handle. He was going to have a use for it, after all.

He sighed and slid deeper into the shadows.

It took Rawlegs only minutes to duck, weave and slither his way to the rear of the sheriff's office, his footsteps falling confidently to every inch of the dirt he had trodden, kicked, washed from his skin and spat from between his teeth (when he had teeth!) for the better part of his life. Not a twist of it he did not know. All second nature.

Not so what he had in mind once through that back door there to Sheriff Simmons's private quarters, sneaking into the shadows far end of the jailhouse and doing his best to take whoever it was acting turnkey by surprise. Never done it before.

And now, he reminded himself on another gulp and surge of sweat across his shoulders, was no time to get to wondering if he could.

Nine

A dozen fast steps and Rawlegs was out of shadow, across the short distance of the sun's full glare and snuggled into the shade at the side of the door.

He waited, catching his breath, blinking and gulping on the notion that he was probably a whole sight too old for this sort of thing. Only advantage he could lay claim to was his knowledge of the ground.

He knew, for instance, that Simmons was in the bad habit of just never locking his back door – maybe his conscience took refuge in having a guaranteed bolt-hole at all times – and always left the inner door to the jailhouse and office off the latch. Man could get to losing his life because of habit, he reflected.

And then, of course, he knew the ways and wiles of whoever it was happened to be doing turnkey duty; one or other of the only two deputies Simmons could trust – Hank Speak or Charlie Ford. This time of day it would almost certainly be Hank. Charlie would be sleeping off the morning booze.

He gulped again and adjusted his sweaty grip on the axe-handle, his fingers tensed and stiff. Easy does it, he thought, edging a half step closer as he reached with his other hand for the doorknob. Easy . . . the softest click. And it was open.

He waited, took a deep breath, cursed mentally at a trickle of irritating sweat, listened. Nothing, save the slow tick of a clock from somewhere in the room.

He moved again, this time sliding across the threshold and closing the door softly behind him in less time than it took for him to swallow and catch his next breath.

So far, so good, he thought, blinking quickly as he adjusted his sight to the softer, gloomier light. Room had not changed since his last visit for a Yuletide toast with Simmons and his deputies. Your good health, Sheriff, he smiled silently to himself, and crossed the room to the inner door.

He waited again, his thoughts spinning for a moment to Abigail, the smoke-hazed, shadow-steeped bar at the saloon, Simmons's eyes searching. . . . He blinked, almost grunted, stifled the temptation and licked slowly at his lips.

No sounds from the office or the jailhouse. Maybe he was getting lucky. Steady, this was no time to push it.

He eased the inner door fully open and sidled into the dark confines of the office, easing himself as tight and close as he could to the tall bulk of the rifle cabinet.

Wait, listen, watch.

Lines of cells to his right, McAdams sprawled on the bunk in the second of three; sheriff's desk ahead – papers, half-empty bottle, glasses, a tin plate, lantern – and beyond that a scrubbed table, Hank Speak at this end of it, seated with his back to

Rawlegs, his head and concentration deep in the pages of a newspaper.

Now for the really difficult part, thought the old man on a parched swallow: how to cross from here to the table, coming up on Hank soft as a mouse, put him firmly to sleep, grab the cell keys and free McAdams, all in the space and time it took to think it. Simple!

He watched the deputy, wondering just how far down the page Hank's reading had taken him. Maybe Hank was a slow reader. He weighed the axe-handle, suddenly a deal heavier in his grip.

No time now to be debating too long on this, he thought, stiffening. Time to shift, do it, trust to luck, and to hell with the consequences. Miss Abi would be waiting on him.

Rawlegs had figured for it taking eight steps to cross from the cabinet to the table. He would raise the handle on the sixth and have it scything air in its thrust for maximum impact on the seventh. All over by the eighth. Hank would have heard nothing, seen nothing and be slumped across the news pages in no time at all. A matter of seconds.

Do it!

He caught the merest flicker of a movement in the cell as he passed into his fifth step. McAdams stirring in his doze? Had he spotted Rawlegs? Hell, surely he would have the good sense to stay silent.

Hank Speak had made to turn a page of the newspaper on Rawlegs' sixth step – but it was to be one he never got to seeing in that particular edition.

The newspaper crackled, Hank shifted a boot, might have thought to scrape his chair back from the table, might have seen a headline blur and lift from the page as if taking flight, but never got to the columns of text as the axe-handle crashed across the back of his head and, with barely more than a stifled moan, he collapsed across the table with a thud.

'Don't ask no questions, mister,' gasped Rawlegs, slipping the ring of keys from Hank's belt and crossing to McAdams, staring wide-eyed behind bars. 'There ain't time for nothin' save gettin' yuh outa here. Grab yuhr gunbelt and help y'self to a Winchester from that cabinet. You'll find a horse saddled up and ready to ride back of the livery. Get there fast. Blacksmith's waitin' on yuh. He's a friend of mine. After that. . . . Make yuh own choices. Now move!'

He opened up the cell, watched McAdams disappear into Simmons's private quarters, heard the click of a door, then collected the axe-handle and followed.

Town hardly seemed to have stirred, he thought, seconds later as he slipped the handle out of sight at the back of the saddlery and crossed casually to the street shadows.

He fidgeted unnecessarily with the buckboard team's tack, checked the wagon's wheels and axles for the tenth time in as many minutes, paused, appeared to relax in close examination of the bowl of his pipe, and finally put a match to it, his tight, worried gaze disappearing behind a cloud of smoke.

Hell, how long to give her, he wondered, his eyes narrowed on the batwings to the bar? How long before he dreamed up some excuse to step through them and call across to Miss Abi as how he was all set to leave soon as she was good and ready. Or would that be the wrong move? Might not sit well with Bart Simmons; might just get to sparking the worst side of him. But, damn it, standing here waiting, watching. . . . And how long before Hank Speak came to and raised the roof on the springing of McAdams?

Rawlegs sighed, fidgeted, blew a thicker cloud of smoke, scuffed a boot through the dirt and leaned against the wagon. Could be, of course, he pondered, that Miss Abi was handling the situation just as she had planned. Never be surprised in a woman of her wilful nature and determination on what she might come to next. Always been the same, even as a youngster. That time out at the Parkers' hoedown, for example. . . .

'Sonofa-goddamn-bitch,' murmured Rawlegs, his gaze suddenly wide and incredulous in the smoke cloud as he watched Simmons's second deputy, Charlie Ford, push open the batwings with a wide-armed flourish, stride to the edge of the shaded boardwalk, blink on the glare, belch loudly, adjust his hat, and step into the street – heading directly for the jailhouse.

'Heck!' mouthed Rawlegs, running a hand over his suddenly sweat-lined face. No time for much in the way of debate from here on. It was going to take Charlie just five minutes to reach the jail, discover Hank and the empty cell and spread himself back to the street like a tornado, all arms and legs, shouting and yelling.

Five minutes.

Rawlegs climbed as casually as his shaking limbs

would permit to the buckboard seat, settled himself and gathered the reins.

Charlie had crossed the street, reached the steps to the sheriff's office, paused as he brushed at an annoying fly, and stepped briskly to the door.

Rawlegs swallowed. Give it another minute, two at most. He clicked his tongue to the team, snapped the reins and eased to the slow, creaking trundle. He would bring the outfit to the front of the saloon, facing the batwings. All Miss Abi would need to do. . . .

Hold it, Charlie was back on the boardwalk, the door standing open behind him, a pale, drawn look masking his face, his eyes wide and bulging, mouth working soundlessly. Only a matter of time though, thought Rawlegs.

'Jail's been hit!' came the shouted roar at last, as Charlie tumbled to the street. 'Jail's been hit! Prisoner's escaped! Yuh hear that? Jail's been hit!'

It took only seconds for bodies to appear as if conjured out of air.

Miras Coutts and a clutter of customers shoved and pushed their way from the store to the board-walk. The batwings creaked and swung wide to the bulk of Joe Heane, a cloth spread at his shoulder, another still in his hands, his apron flapping at his knees as the drinkers stumbled and jostled from the bar.

'Is the end nigh?' spluttered a staggering old soak, wobbling his way to the street.

'Jail's been hit! Prisoner's escaped!' yelled Charlie at the top of his voice, the street dust beginning to swarm to his scuffing steps.

A woman screamed from a high window. Joe

Heane dropped the cloth and stepped on it. A youngster scurried between Miras Coutts's legs and headed for the candy jar. A handful of bar girls flounced to the side of the buckboard and began to giggle.

'The end is nigh!' croaked the soak again. 'Somebody get me a drink!'

Rawlegs gulped on a throat tight with clinging dirt, his gaze watering in the strain of watching, squinting into the dark bar, for a sight of Abigail. Where in hell was she? Where was Simmons?

'Somebody get the sheriff,' came a shout.

Charlie straddled the street, turning left, right, full circle, eyes whitening like moons, the sweat flying from his face. 'Don't nobody go nowhere,' he yelled. 'Fella might be anywhere.'

A woman screamed again. The bar girls began to panic. Rawlegs took the strain as the buckboard team grew restless.

'Where's Simmons?' shouted a man.

A single shot whined and screamed to the high blue sky. 'He's right here!' growled the sheriff, pushing his way through the bar-room mob to the front of the boardwalk. 'Now, just what in hell's name is goin' on here? Charlie, will yuh quit prancin' like a mountain bear and get your butt here? And you, all of yuh, stand back. Back! And cut out that shoutin', yuh hear?'

Rawlegs sighed. She was there – Miss Abigail, right behind Simmons, the scarf at her neck, a slow, satisfied smile dancing at her lips. She winked as she accepted Rawlegs' help to the buckboard seat.

'No unseemly haste,' she murmured softly, adjusting the folds of her dress across her knees. 'Don't make it that obvious, but I think we're all through here, don't you?'

She nodded politely, almost demurely, to Sheriff Simmons.

Ten

The east wind whipping through the Washback was there again at dusk on that day – bit like a ragbag drifter reminding you he was still about, Rawlegs had thought – but it had been no natural dust cloud gathered in the grip of it that had finally held his attention as he stepped from the paddock to the homestead veranda at Abigail's call to wash-up for supper.

Nothing like a wind-whipped cloud, he reckoned, peering hard through the deepening gloom. Dust cloud moving that fast, sharp and straight as a plucked arrow, could only be riders.

'I figure for us havin' company,' he called to the lantern glow beyond the open door to the living-room. 'Three riders. And they ain't for hangin' about.'

'Moldoon's men? frowned Abigail, coming to Rawlegs' side, her hands working anxiously in the cloth she was holding.

'Wouldn't think so. Not yet. No, I'd say more like Sheriff Simmons and his deputies in a lather.'

'Oh, dear,' murmured Abigail. 'I hope that doesn't mean—'

'He ain't got nothin' on us, miss. Not unless I didn't hit Hank Speak hard enough!' Rawlegs grunted and scratched his stubbled chin. 'Best if I do the talkin', I reckon.'

'Suppose they've taken Mr McAdams prisoner again. Perhaps he didn't get away. Perhaps something went wrong at the livery. Supposing—'

'Bet my boots to a scoop of sand as how Simmons ain't seen so much as a hair of his prisoner.' Rawlegs grunted again and swallowed. 'Find out soon enough, shan't we?'

'Supper's comin' to the table, so I'd appreciate yuh makin' this real fast, Bart Simmons. I ain't for missin' out on Miss Abi's cookin'. What's on yuh mind?'

Rawlegs' gaze swept quickly across the faces of the riders, their shapes in half silhouette against the thickening dust, the wind whipping and chattering at their long coats.

Charlie Ford to his left, his eyes as wide and bulging as ever, the smell of sweat and liquor drifting from his clothes. Bart Simmons, centre, his expression tense, stare fixed, hands tight to the reins; fellow with a lot on his mind, mused Rawlegs, tightening his lips to hide a soft smile to himself. And, to the right, Hank Speak, a bandage showing beneath the set of his hat, his face pale and empty, gaze vacant and lost to someplace else; as if, thought Rawlegs, somebody had made him see stars.

'McAdams broke jail,' said Simmons flatly.

'So it seems,' grinned Rawlegs. 'Mite careless, weren't yuh? Not concentratin', or somethin?'

Simmons glanced quickly at Abigail Grey. 'Don't

fret. We'll bring him in,' he went on. 'He won't get far.'

'Wouldn't bet to that,' said Rawlegs casually. 'Very resourceful fella yuh got there. Washback won't trouble him none. Army trained.'

Charlie Ford scowled but held his tongue. Hank simply gazed. Bart Simmons shifted uncomfortably.

'Now just who would yuh figure would want to spring a man like McAdams?' asked Rawlegs, a touch of mockery in his voice. 'Apart from m'self, o'course, who reckoned he shouldn't have been jailed in the first place.'

'You were in town,' snapped Simmons.

'Sure I was. Waitin' on Miss Abi here.' Rawlegs' gaze narrowed. 'Yuh see anythin' of who gave yuh cause for that bandage, Hank?'

Hank simply shrugged.

'There yuh are, then,' said Rawlegs, thrusting his hands to his trousers pockets. 'Could've been anybody, couldn't it? Who's to say?'

'Chances are McAdams'll make his way here,' said Simmons bluntly. 'And don't argue other. I ain't that big a fool. He'll be here, sooner or later, so yuh'd best know I'll be watchin' the place, round the clock, day and night. Yuh got that? McAdams shows here, I'll know. And next time it'll be shootin' on sight.' His gaze settled on Abigail. 'Suggest yuh take good care, Miss Abi. We got some unfinished business to get to sometime.'

'Don't bank on it,' croaked Rawlegs.

Simmons reined his mount to the teeth of the wind and the deepening night. 'Supper smells real good, miss,' he called. 'Shame I can't join yuh. Next time, maybe.'

'And I wouldn't bet on that neither!' growled Rawlegs.

'Sonofabitch! There ain't another word for him,' grumbled Rawlegs, his flushed, angry face disappearing in a shroud of pipe smoke. 'I ain't for mixin' words where that so-called sheriff's concerned.' He wafted a hand to clear the smoke and leaned back in his chair at the supper-table. 'Still, shouldn't be speakin' that way after such a fine meal. Sorry.'

Abigail relaxed in the chair facing the old man. 'But he means what he says, doesn't he? He will be watching. And he will shoot on sight.'

Rawlegs sighed. 'He will – if he gets close enough, which I doubt.'

'If Mr McAdams has got any sense he'll keep riding while he has the chance.'

'Yuh reckon for him doin' that – Sam Pooley's best friend? No, miss, that's the last thing he'll do.'

'But if he shows his face here. . . . And then there's Moldoon. Can't be long before he's back.' Abigail came sharply to her feet. 'There can't be another death here, can there? No spread, no land, however big, is worth it. Perhaps it really would be better for everyone, before there's any more killing, if I—'

'No!' said Rawlegs, a clenched fist crashing to the table. 'Don't even think it, miss. That's just the way Moldoon wants yuh to get to feelin'. He's bankin' on it. Hell, miss, don't let's get to doin' it for him! We ain't through yet. Not by a long shot we ain't.'

Trouble was, thought Rawlegs, later when the night had closed in, the supper-table been cleared, the lanterns doused and Abigail retired to her room, neither was Stove Moldoon, and nor would he so much as reckon on being all through until he had moved his men to the town of Resolute and put the Pooley spread as good as under siege. Moldoon's 'all through' meant when Moldoon had taken what he wanted.

He had sighed, grunted, muttered to himself and stepped quietly to the veranda for a last smoke before turning in to the homestead spare room Abigail was insisting on him taking, when he figured on checking out the bunkhouse and battening it down against the whipping wind.

'Get to fixin' them loose windows one of these days . . . that door too,' he was murmuring as he leaned to the buffeting wind in his stride across the paddock.

Sure enough, there was a window only part latched, and it would be only a matter of time before that door slipped its broken bolt, and one of these days that end roof section. . . .

'Rawlegs – get yourself in here and don't make a sound!'

The voice came out of the darkness on the crack of the twisting, moaning wind.

McAdams was back.

Eleven

Rawlegs tumbled into the pitch blackness of the bunkhouse, the door banging to its broken bolt behind him like a piece of flotsam caught in the swirl of the wind.

A hand settled tight as a manacle on his shoulder.

'All quiet out there?' said McAdams, his piercing gaze moving closer.

'As a mouse,' muttered Rawlegs on a deep swallow.

'No visitors?'

'Not yet. Just give it time.'

McAdams grunted and relaxed. 'Some break-out yuh pulled back there at the jail,' he grinned. 'I gotta thank yuh.'

'Think nothin' of it,' hissed Rawlegs on another long swallow. 'And don't mention it! More I think about it now. . . . Miss Abi's idea. Some woman, eh? Her yuh gotta really thank.' The old man flexed his shoulders. 'Anyhow yuh ain't penned no more; that's what it was all about. But I gotta tell yuh—'

'I can guess,' said McAdams briskly. 'Simmons is goin' to keep a round-the-clock watch on this place. Figured as much.'

'And it's only goin' to be a matter of time before Moldoon hits town again – a whole army of his side-kicks ridin' on his tail.' Rawlegs smacked his lips. 'I'm all for fightin' my corner, mister, and I'll stand to Miss Abi to the last, but I gotta tell yuh minute Moldoon gets to playin' ugly with that amount of guns standin' to him, well – heck, I'm goin' to have to look to Miss Abi first.' He paused, the wind lifting to an echoing howl beyond the bunkhouse. 'So what do we do now? Yuh got a plan?'

'Yuh sit tight here, that's for sure,' said McAdams. 'Don't leave the place, not for nothin'.'

'And yourself?'

'I'll be around.'

'Sure,' began Rawlegs, 'but what about—?'

But by then the man had slipped deep into the shadows and there was suddenly neither sight nor sound of him.

Nothing save the whine of the wind and the door creaking sadly on its broken bolt.

They were out there, two of them, Charlie Ford and a gravel-faced, unshaven drunk by the name of Stamps, far side of the low bluff, just off the town trail.

'Been there since sun-up,' murmured Rawlegs, squinting into the early brightness from the home-stead veranda on a calmer, clearer morning. 'Just sittin' there, watchin'.' He grunted as Abigail came closer to his side.

'Simmons is scrapin' the barrel some recruitin' the likes of Stamps,' he went on, raising a hand to shield his eyes. 'Be lucky if he survives 'til noon before his thirst gets the better of him!'

'Nothin' of Mr McAdams?' said Abigail.

'Nothin', and no sayin' where he's headed or what he's plannin'. One minute he was there last night in the bunkhouse, next he was gone. No point in followin'. He knows where we are. Ain't goin' no place, are we? And I don't think he is neither.'

'You mean we just wait?' frowned Abigail. 'Do nothing? Hand the initiative to Moldoon.'

'I know, miss, t'ain't in my nature neither.'

'Surely there must be somethin' we can do?'

Rawlegs ran a hand over his chin. 'Well, miss, right now I'd opt for a makin' of fresh coffee if yuh got the time.'

'Time enough for that!' smiled Abigail. 'You just keep your eyes on what's happenin' out there.'

And he did – through a whole pot of coffee, down to the very dregs, until well past the searing heat of noon and the hour when Charlie Ford and Stamps retired to rest in the cooler shade of a rocky outcrop; until the shadows began to lengthen again and Abigail tended to the chores for supper and he finally got to thinking he would do his rounds, look to the stock, check out the buildings, go shift that hay pile in the big barn, water up, settle the place in readiness against the return of that mean, whipping Washback wind.

He was all through at the barn and on his way to check out the water-troughs when the sudden gleam and flash of light at the bluff drew his attention and halted him where he stood at the far end of the sprawling corral.

More riders joining up with Ford and Stamps. Ben Morton, Sleeks Hooper, Clyde Carter, Marty

Neal ... a handful of choice town scum, thought Rawlegs, counting them in. So what was this, the night watch? They plan on setting up camp there? Mite slow in their thinking, surely, if they reckoned on McAdams showing his face to that amount of armoury.

Or had Simmons dreamed up some other nasty scheme? Maybe he had heard from Moldoon. Perhaps there had been a message. Orders.

'Yeah,' murmured Rawlegs to himself, 'mebbe he's under orders. . . .'

And maybe the time had come for Simmons to act on them.

The old man flicked his gaze anxiously to the homestead, the deserted veranda, chimney smoke twisting to the first touch of the breeze. Best get back to Miss Abi, he thought, beginning to move. Get her to batten down, load up the shotguns.

You could never be too careful, not where Simmons was concerned, and definitely not when he had come to putting the likes of Sleeks Hooper on the payroll.

He had turned his back on the corral, quickened his stride to the homestead and was already squirming at the trickle of a cold sweat across his shoulders, when he stopped, listened to the suddenly pounding beat of hoofs behind him, and swung round to stare wide-eyed at the line of riders bearing down on him like something out of a hell-fire.

The sounds thudded through his head, spinning and reeling his thoughts to a jumble. Dust burned across his eyes. His limbs were suddenly heavy, his legs rooted to the paddock dirt as if grown there. He shouted a stream of curses, but nothing of them was heard against the thunderous beat of hoofs.

It was only seconds then before the first of the riders – a leering, sneering Sleeks Hooper – had thrust the flanks of his mount across Rawlegs' chest, flinging the old man to the ground as if no more than a twig of frail scrub.

Rawlegs wiped a smear of blood from his eyes, struggled to his knees, shouting curses between spitting dirt from his mouth, and watched the riders slither their mounts to a halt, rein them round to face him again and pound forward in another shuddering drive.

Rawlegs got to his feet, swaying, arms reaching for balance, eyes round and cold as stones in his dust-caked face, the sweat soaking through his shirt, and stumbled towards the corral.

The riders whooped, jeered, taunted, giving the old man his head for a moment before breaking the line as Clyde Carter rounded him up like a loose steer.

He stumbled, staggered headlong, arms outstretched, blood and sweat flying, hit the ground face down, groaned and winced as hoofs skimmed across his legs, grazed his ankles and threatened, he was sure, to stamp him to death.

'Petticoat spread ain't such a healthy place to be, is it, old-timer?' sneered Hooper, circling his mount round Rawlegs.

'Sure goin' to need a smooth hand to yuh brow tonight, eh?' cracked Clyde Carter. 'Woman up there got a soft touch, has she?'

'Well, mebbe we'll go see for ourselves when we're

all done here,' whooped Ben Morton. 'How about that, old man?'

Rawlegs cursed, spat, squirmed in the dirt, his gaze half blinded by the swirling dust, trickling blood and sweat.

'Marty, Clyde – you go pull that corral apart, will yuh?' yelled Hooper. 'Let's do just like Mr Simmons asked, eh? Let's mess the place up some!'

The riders whooped, yelled. Mounts snorted, whinnied. Hoofs pounded. Tack jangled, leather cracked.

Dust and dirt whirled, the strengthening wind whipping at it as if joining in the mayhem.

Rawlegs groaned, struggled to make his body work, his blood running cold at the high echoing scream from the homestead. God willing, Miss Abi would stay right where she was, he prayed.

The sickening grind and splinter of crashing timber. . . . Rawlegs groaned again, blinking furiously now for a sight of the corral, seeing its fencing ripped apart, the horses fleeing in a wild panic of flying tails and dancing manes.

'Sonsof-goddamn-bitches!' he cursed, thudding fists to the dirt.

'See how rough it can get, old man?' mouthed Sleeks Hooper. 'And a whole lot worse than this, let me tell yuh. A whole lot worse. So you just make sure yuh start talkin' some sense into that woman's head, eh? You tell her straight – this spread ain't for her. Yuh got that?'

'Go to hell!' spat Rawlegs.

'We're already there, old man! Already there!'

More splintering timbers. Whoops. Snorts. Shouts. Curses.

'And just remember, old fella,' jeered Hooper, 'only reason we're leavin' you alive is so's yuh can get talkin' to that woman. There ain't no other. So yuh get to it – fast – 'cus we're comin' back. Real soon.'

Hooper rounded his mount on a fierce swirl of dust, lifting a dust shroud that clouded the devastation from Rawlegs' view.

It was some minutes then, with the sounds still crashing through his head and his body at the point of breaking, before he heard the crack and snarl of rifle fire from somewhere that might have been a million miles away.

Twelve

The smell of dirt, dust and stale sweat; the taste of blood; the sounds of a wind moaning between timbers; somewhere the tick of a clock; the soft, blurred glow of a lantern among shadows and the oncoming night. The touch of a hand.

'Thank heavens,' murmured Abigail, leaning closer. 'For a moment, there, I was beginning to think. . . . Easy, easy.'

'What the—' Rawlegs blinked, winced, screwed his craggy features against the dull aches, stabbing pains, and pushed himself to one elbow. 'Hell, what in the name of—' He groaned and shuddered.

'Take your time,' urged Abigail, helping the old man sit upright on the bed. 'There's no hurry.'

Rawlegs winced again. 'How'd I get here? What's happenin' out there? What about—?'

'Simmons has gone, most of his men with him. Two of them shot dead at the bluff.'

'Dead? But who got to 'em?'

'Mr McAdams,' said Abigail, arranging the pillows at Rawlegs' back.

'Where'd he spring from? He still here?'

'Doing his best to round up any stock he can track down before it's full dark.'

Rawlegs moaned, fell back on the pillows, and closed his eyes. 'That bad, eh?'

'That bad. They pulled the corral apart, scattered the horses. There isn't a single head left. They shot through most of the water-troughs, wrecked the small barn and one of the out-shacks. Thought at one time they were going to torch the big barn, but Simmons pulled them out when Mr McAdams hit the trail from wherever he'd been hiding. I think he shot Charlie Ford and that fellow Stamps.'

Abigail sighed, looked away for a moment, then slid her hand to Rawlegs' arm. 'You were lucky. A miracle you weren't trampled to death. Mr McAdams brought you in.' She sighed again. 'Thank the Lord you're alive.'

'I get my hands on that sonofabitch sheriff . . .' began Rawlegs, struggling upright again. 'I'm tellin' yuh, Miss Abi, only so much a body can take before. . . .' He winced. 'Hell, I might be gettin' old, but, damnit, I ain't for lettin' Simmons get away with this. Not no how, no way.'

'You're in in no fit state to do anything. And besides, it's almost night. And there's another thing – we're all finished here, washed up. Enough's enough.'

'Oh, no, we ain't, miss,' growled Rawlegs, squirming on the pillows. 'We back down now, and—'

Abigail turned angrily from the bed to the window where the darkness gathered. 'We can't fight against the sort of thing we've just witnessed. How can we? You, me, Mr McAdams against. . . . Lord above knows how many?' She spun round, her gaze wet and glazed. 'This can only end one way – in more killing. Any one of us, perhaps all of us, might be the next to die. And that is a price too high.'

'But, miss, we gotta try—'

'No, Rawlegs, the odds are too great. There's too much at stake. It just isn't worth it.'

'Wouldn't have been Sam Pooley's thinkin',' said the voice from the shadows beyond the lantern glow.

McAdams, dust and sweat-smeared, his clothes grey and blackened with Washback dirt, waited on the edge of the darkness, his piercing gaze like a fixed beam, Winchester crooked in his arm.

'Just as I was about to say,' enthused Rawlegs, struggling higher on his pillows. 'Captain Pooley would've been for fightin' on, not givin' up a thing. Why, damn it, I've heard him say, time and again—'

'Sam is dead,' flared Abigail, her gaze dampening and gleaming on a flood of surface tears, flicking quickly from McAdams to Rawlegs before she turned her back on both of them and stared through the window into the emptiness of the night. 'You sometimes seem to forget that,' she added quietly, folding her arms.

'Ain't nobody forgets—' began Rawlegs.

'We can't turn this into a war, however right we may be. We can't kill and almost certainly be killed.' Abigail brushed self-consciously at a tear. 'Sam wouldn't have wanted that for me. He didn't leave me this spread for my blood, your blood, to be spilled fighting for it.'

'That's true, miss.' said Rawlegs, easing himself from the bed to his feet. 'But he sure as hell didn't leave it to yuh for yuh to go handin' it to a rat like Stove Moldoon for the price of free passage off the

Washback to God knows where. That he surely did not!' He slapped his lips, but could not stifle a wince. 'Weren't thinkin' like yuh are when we took the risks to free McAdams here. We weren't for packin' in then, and, damnit, we ain't now. Are we?'

Abigail turned slowly from the window and stared hard at McAdams. 'What do we have left?' she asked coldly. 'Anything worth having?'

McAdams eased the rifle in his crooked arm. 'Stock's scattered. Take days and more hands than we can raise to round 'em up. Corral's a mess. Can be repaired, but it'll take time. Same goes for the small barn.'

'And you still think we can fight on?' mocked Abigail.

'Yes, miss, I do.'

'In spite of the fact that it's almost certain those men will be back, probably with Moldoon's men to help them, and particularly so in view of the fact that you, Mr McAdams, shot Charlie Ford and Stamps. I can't see Simmons taking that lyin' down, can you? And when they do come back. . . .'

Abigail dropped her arms to her sides and crossed the room to the door, brushing briskly past McAdams, turned and stared at the two men. 'I do not regret for one minute taking the chance we did to free you, Mr McAdams. I just hope you will put that freedom to good use and ride out of here at first light. Rawlegs and myself will manage – we shall be in no danger, because tomorrow I shall ride into Resolute and arrange for a message of acceptance of an offer to sell the spread to be forwarded to Moldoon.' She tossed her hair defiantly across her shoulders. 'And now I will bid you both goodnight.'

Rawlegs watched in silence as Abigail crossed the living area to her own bedroom, entered it and closed the door firmly behind her.

'And she'll do just that if she's of a mind,' he murmured, easing painfully back to the bed. 'So what we goin' to do now, Lieutenant McAdams? What would yuh figure for Captain Pooley doin'? Best get to thinkin', 'cus I got a terrible feelin' time's runnin' out on us.'

Rawlegs had no real idea of just how much time had run out through that night, save that there had been enough to bring up a first touch of light in the east when he woke to the sound of approaching riders, the jangle of tack and the crack of worn leather.

Bart Simmons, Sleeks Hooper and Clyde Carter were already reining to a halt, the damp dawn air glistening like a dew on their stubbled chins, their eyes red-rimmed and tired, as he stumbled to the homestead veranda, blinked and waited for the sheriff to ease his mount closer.

'Don't know how yuh got the gall to ride in here, Bart Simmons, after what you and your scumbag sidekicks did,' the old man growled, wincing on the stabs of pain in his limbs. 'Two bits to a bad boot I'd sure as hell whip the hide off yuh if it weren't—'

'All right, all right,' spat Simmons, 'yuh said enough, old-timer. We ain't for takin' any note of it, and yuh take my advice yuh'll count yourself lucky you're still breathin'. That fella McAdams about?'

'Do yuh see him? No, yuh don't, so he ain't!'

'There'll be no hangin' him now,' said Simmons, his hands twisting through reins. 'It'll be shootin' on sight for the deaths of Charlie Ford and Stamps. Yuh got that? See as he gets to hear. Meantime, yuh go stir Miss Abigail.'

'The hell I will!' snapped Rawlegs, glancing quickly beyond Simmons and the others for a sight of McAdams.

'Suit yourself,' said Simmons. 'Sleeks, go wake the woman,' he ordered, turning to the sidekick.

'You hold it right there,' spluttered Rawlegs. 'Ain't nobody crossin' this threshold, least of all to Miss Abi's room, 'ceptin' over my dead body.'

'You'll be dead sure enough, time we've finished,' drawled Simmons. 'Sleeks. . . .'

'What yuh want with her?' croaked Rawlegs.

'Wanted for aidin' and abettin', and probably organizin', the escape of a prisoner from my jail. And don't you go denyin' it.'

'That was my doin',' blustered Rawlegs, backing to the homestead door. 'I put Hank to sleep, released McAdams. It was me at the jail.'

'I know that,' sighed Simmons. 'Found that axe-handle yuh ain't paid for yet, didn't I? T'ain't you I'm interested in, old man. It's Miss Abigail.' He leaned forward in the saddle, his eyes narrowed to dark slits on the thin dawn light. 'I'm takin' her into town. I want her and so does Moldoon. Now, you goin' to let us get to this the quiet way, or is Sleeks here goin' to have to get nasty?'

Simmons spat fiercely. 'Don't see yuh friend McAdams around. He deserted yuh or somethin'?' He spat again and grinned. 'Sleeks, get to it. . . .'

Thirteen

'I seen it. You seen it. Damnit, more than half the town seen it. And them as didn't see it sure as hell got to hear of it soon enough. So what we goin' to do about it, that's what I want to know?'

Miras Coutts settled his elbows on the corner table in the bar of Joe Heane's saloon and stared long and hard into the proprietor's face.

'Well,' he hissed, his eyes bulging, 'what yuh got to say? Got to do somethin', ain't we? Hell, can't leave Miss Abigail in Simmons's hands. No sayin' what that thick head might get to? And how come he brought her in like he did? What's the charge?'

'Connivin' in the escape of that prisoner Simmons was holdin',' said Heane, fingering an empty glass absent-mindedly.

'Can't prove it, can he?'

' 'Course he can't. Don't have to, does he? And in any case, prisoner ain't the real concern. Stove Moldoon's at the root of this, him and his wantin' to buy out Miss Abi's spread. Simmons figures he's doin' Moldoon a favour.'

'Well, now,' huffed Coutts, 'we'll see about that, won't we?'

Heane pushed the glass from his reach and leaned back in his chair. 'Oh, sure,' he drawled with a shrug. 'You, me, maybe a half-dozen of us ranged against the likes of Sleeks Hooper, Clyde Carter and the rest of the town scum, not to mention Moldoon's men when he gets here with them. Oh, sure. . . . You heard what happened out the Pooley spread yesterday?'

'I heard,' said the storekeeper. 'Charlie Ford and Stamps dead – shot by that fella McAdams so they say. Good riddance too, if you ask me. They get to terrorizin' folk and they pay a high price.'

'Maybe, but yuh don't figure for Simmons takin' that lightly, do yuh? 'Course he won't. He brings in Miss Abi and he's holdin' all the cards, ain't he? McAdams'll make a move for her, and the woman'll probably finish up so damned scared she'll sell out to Moldoon whatever the price – if she ain't already made up her mind to do just that.'

'Don't know about you, Joe,' said Coutts, 'but I ain't much for lettin' that happen. Half step short of robbery, ain't it? Hell, why should a fella like Moldoon—'

'I hear yuh, Miras,' said Heane, holding up a hand to halt him, 'loud and clear, but I ain't for comin' to a single notion as to how you're goin' to stop him. And, truth of it, neither are you.'

The storekeeper grunted and drummed his fingers on the table. 'Anybody seen Rawlegs since Simmons brought the woman in?' he murmured.

'I'd reckon for him still bein' out on the spread – guardin' whatever there is left of it worth watchin' over. What else can he do?'

'And where's McAdams?'

'Now that,' said Heane, leaning closer, his eyes narrowing, 'is somethin' else entirely, ain't it?'

Well, thought Rawlegs, pacing the length of the homestead veranda yet again, one hand shielding his gaze against the sun's glare as he scanned the empty paddock to the Washback trail, and just where in tarnation was the fellow?

Damn it, McAdams must surely have seen Simmons and his men ride in; must have seen them ride out again with Miss Abi between them; must have realized Simmons was taking her in. He could hardly have hidden himself that deep.

So how come he had made no move, done nothing? Or was it that he had done just what Miss Abi had suggested – pulled out and kept right on going? No, not the one-time army man; it would be out of character.

Rawlegs turned and paced back through the shadows. Give him another hour, he reckoned. Well, maybe until midday. After that.... He halted, stared despairingly over the broken corral, the small barn with its shattered doors, splintered timbers, the holed water-troughs; swallowed on the silence, the emptiness, the stray drift of brush caught in the whisper of a breeze.

What should he do? Walk away from it all, get into town, do the best he could by Miss Abi? What the hell good could he do out here, anyhow, one man on his own? Maybe he could raise some help. Barney at the livery; Miras Coutts; Joe Heane. Anybody willing enough. Or fool enough to stand up to murdering guns!

Or maybe he could talk some sense into Stove

Moldoon. Sure – open his mouth on a dozen words before somebody filled it with lead!

'What the hell!' he cursed, spitting deep into the dirt. He would give it until noon and then go face Simmons.

'So how come we get to wet-nursin' the lame dog out there? Can't say I'm much for it.' Ben Morton aimed a curving fount of spittle across the dirt and eased his body deeper into the lean shade at the bluff. He squinted towards the curl of smoke at the distant homestead.

'Old man's still pacin' that veranda. Wearin' his boots out.'

'T'ain't the old man who bothers me,' said Marty Neale from the other side of the shade, his face wet with sweat. 'It's that sonofabitch who did for Charlie Ford and Stamps. Fella who took out Moldoon's men. Who the hell is he, anyhow?'

'Name's McAdams, one-time friend of that fella Pooley.' Morton targeted another line of spittle. 'He ain't nobody. Don't fidget me none.'

'Fella gets to leavin' dead bodies round him the way he does, sure in hell fidgets me! Who's he got lined up next? Way we messed up that spread down there, might be any one of us.'

Morton stretched his long legs. 'Well, now,' he drawled, tipping his hat against the glare, 'we could always get to givin' the fella some good reason to come out of wherever he's holed-up. 'Stead of this wet-nursin' and just watchin', we could get down there, have ourselves some fun with the old man, get him dancin' to lead, and wait for Mr McAdams to crawl out of the woodwork. How's that appeal to yuh?'

'Simmons said to just watch the place. Make sure Rawlegs stays right where he is. I ain't much for tanglin', and I sure ain't for roustin' no sight of McAdams.'

'Suit yourself,' said Morton, leaning back. 'I ain't fussed, 'cept when I get to thinkin' of Simmons and Sleeks with that Grey woman all to themselves. How come we draw the short straw? And where's Clyde?'

'Last I seen of Clyde he was sleepin' it off. . . .' Neale's words trailed away to a whisper as he wiped a hand over his face. 'Yuh hear that?' he murmured.

'Hear what?'

'Somethin' out there. Other side them boulders.'

'Gopher,' grunted Morton. 'Maybe a snake.'

'Snake don't make that noise. And this ain't gopher country.' Neale fell silent, listening, sweating. Yuh hear it now?' he hissed.

'No, don't hear a thing, save for yuh frettin'.'

'Well, I do,' croaked Neale. 'I'm takin' a look. Yuh cover me. Right?'

'Right,' said Morton, without moving.

He heard Neale crawl away; heard him slip his Colt clear of leather, the click of the hammer; heard him pause, take a breath, crawl on.

That was the trouble with Marty, he thought, closing his eyes; Marty was always fidgeting. Could never sit still long enough to crease his pants, let alone wear them thin. Smart with a gun, fast too, but when it came to his nerves, hell, they were shredded thinner than brushwood in a drought. Marty heard things most men never would. It was just the way of the fellow.

'Well,' said Morton, 'what yuh see? Anythin' out there?'

No answer.

'Yuh hear me? I said anythin' out there?'

Silence.

'What yuh spot – a baskin' rattler? Yuh leave it well alone, yuh hear!'

Morton smiled softly to himself.

Silence. Not a movement. Not a sound.

'Marty, yuh still there? How far yuh figure on crawlin' – clear across the Washback or somethin'?'

It was not until Ben Morton had finally stirred himself, settled his hat, spat and wiped the sweat from his neck, that his gaze narrowed and began to probe, and that first prickling hint of a warning instinct that marks out the gunslinger niggled across his back.

'Marty?' he called, but this time on no more than a hissing whisper.

Silence.

He slewed the back of his hand across his mouth, dropped to his knees and crawled on all-fours through the tracks of Marty Neale, scuff by scuff, yard by yard, deeper into shadow, until he halted, gasped and, without needing to look down to what his fingers had slithered into, shuddered at the touch.

Marty's blood was still warm.

Fourteen

'Well, yuh with me, or ain't yuh? Got to do somethin'.
Me, I'm all for fightin'.' Miras Coutts blinked on the
billowing curls of smoke from the livery forge and
watched anxiously as Barney Todds hammered out
a length of white-hot iron. 'What yuh say?' he added,
behind a spluttered cough.

'I say we do what we can by Miss Abi,' said the
blacksmith, shaking the sweat from his jowls. 'Sure
I do. Only decent thing to do, but I ain't for rushin'
into it. We got to think it through.' His muscles
rippled under another onslaught with the hammer.

'Ain't that much to think through, is there? I
mean, somebody's got to look to her spread for one
thing. Give that old fool, Rawlegs, a helpin' hand.
Then we gotta do somethin' about gettin' Miss Abi
outa that damned jail. And when we done that—'

'Whoa! Ease up there some, will yuh?' grinned
Todds. 'Who are the folk doin' all this? Some sorta
army? How many we lookin' to? Who we got with
us? Where, when, how? And you talked yet to
McAdams? Do yuh know where he is?'

The storekeeper wafted aside more billowing

smoke. 'Reckon we can look to a half-dozen of us so far. There'll be more, you see, once word gets about.'

'Yeah,' said Todds, 'once word gets about *and Simmons gets to hear it!* Yuh thought of that? Sheriff's playin' a big stake here. Can't afford any mistakes, can he? Anybody crosses him, looks to be upsettin' the pan, and – wham! – he's goin' to be there. And believe me, Miras, the lead will spread fast.'

'Well,' began Coutts, brushing ash from his coat, 'yuh could be right. But I still say—'

'We need to talk to McAdams, don't we? He's the one callin' the other half of the shots round here. Maybe he's got some sorta plan in mind. Or maybe—'

It was in that moment, as the smoke at the forge billowed to a thicker cloud, hovered and began to clear slowly on the drift of a soft afternoon breeze, that the scuff of tired hoofs at the far end of the street to the Washback trail drew the attention of Miras Coutts and the blacksmith.

Coutts rubbed at his eyes, as if not quite believing what he was seeing. Barney Todds eased the hammer to its resting place on the forge and simply stared at the sight of Ben Morton, slumped on his mount and bleeding bad from a knife wound at his shoulder, trailing Marty Neale's horse on a loose line behind him, the man's body slung across it like a sad, sagging sack of flour.

'Yuh see that . . .?' murmured Coutts. 'What in the name of hell happened there?'

'I'd figure that for bein' McAdams's handiwork,' said Todds. 'Oh, yes, that I would.'

The approach of the horses had roused Hank

Speak from his rocker on the porch fronting the sheriff's office and sent him scurrying in search of Simmons.

Joe Heane had pushed open the batwings at the saloon and stepped like a man in a sleep to the boardwalk, a scattering of curious but strangely silent drinkers and bar girls following him.

'I'll be damned,' said a man watching from the shadows on the opposite side of the street.

'Marty Neale,' hissed another. 'Somebody's cut the scumbag's throat.'

'Trailin' in there from the Pooley spread.'

'Hell, yuh figure that for bein' . . . Oh, hell.'

'Best go get Doc Raines.'

'Undertaker along of him. . . .'

Simmons closed the door to his office, paused a moment, his gaze ranging the street as if devouring it, then moved slowly to the steps of the boardwalk, signalled for Hank to guide Morton's mount to the hitching rail, and stared for a long half-minute at Marty Neale's bloodstained body.

Sleeks Hooper sidled to the sheriff's side. Clyde Carter ambled out of the shadows at the rear of the office.

Barney Todds' hand reached instinctively for the handle of his hammer. 'Yuh still all for fightin' this through, Miras?' he asked quietly. 'Or do yuh figure for somebody bein' a whole heap of steps ahead of us?'

There was a tense, almost painful silence settled over Resolute later that day when Rawlegs, sneaking in on the back trail from the north, finally reached the alley at the rear of the saloon and tapped carefully on the door to Joe Heane's private room.

Five minutes and a measure of Joe's best whiskey later and he was staring wide-eyed and grey at the gills into Joe's troubled face.

'I'm tellin' yuh straight up, Simmons is seethin' somethin' fit to boil his blood,' said the bar-keeper, pouring another measure. 'That fella McAdams has pulled one right over him again, ain't he? First, he gets clear of jail – easy as pluckin' berries, thanks to you and Miss Abi – then he takes out Charlie Ford and Stamps, and now, damnit, smart as new boots and in broad daylight too, he cuts Marty Neale's throat and leaves Ben Morton of no use to nobody for days, mebbe weeks. Tell me if that ain't prickin' a sheriff's pride!'

'And I never saw, never heard a thing,' murmured Rawlegs. 'Not a sound, not a shadow.'

' 'Course yuh didn't. Weren't meant to, were yuh? McAdams is for workin' alone, and I'd figure for him keepin' it that way.'

'Mebbe,' sighed Rawlegs, 'but that don't change the fact that he's one man on his own. So he may take out Simmons's men – one by one, real soft and slow – but that ain't helpin' Miss Abi right now, and it sure as hell ain't takin' no account of Moldoon and the guns he'll be ridin' in here any minute.'

'Miras is for raisin' as many as he can to stand to Miss Abi,' said Joe with a resigned shrug of his shoulders. 'Don't amount to much, though.'

Rawlegs pushed at the brim of his hat. 'Might come to there bein' no need if Miss Abi keeps to her promise – said as how she was for giving the nod to Moldoon to make an offer.'

'Won't be worth the paper it's writ on,' grunted Joe.

'Tell *her* that! Got some notion in her head there's been enough killin'. So there has, but that don't bother Moldoon one hoot.'

Joe finished his drink. 'Best get back to the bar. You're welcome to stay, but I wouldn't be in a hurry to show yuh face around town. What yuh plannin'? Gettin' back to the spread?'

'Later, later,' said Rawlegs thoughtfully. 'I gotta see Miss Abi first.'

'Hell, you're takin' a risk there! Mood Simmons is in, he'd like as not measure yuh for a pine box soon as look at yuh.'

'Well, mebbe he will at that. Mebbe. . . . See yuh around, Joe. Thanks for the drink.'

Joe waited until Rawlegs had slipped back to the alley and closed the door softly behind him before tossing a clean cloth to his shoulder, tightening the apron at his waist and heading for the saloon where there was already a hushed, mournful silence among the drinkers.

Fitting for a funeral wake, he thought, with another resigned shrug.

It took Rawlegs only minutes to work his way towards the back of the jailhouse and the door he knew was never locked.

Lord above knew what crazy notion he had running round his mind for getting to see Abigail where she was being held, how she might be sprung, if Simmons might be reasoned with – but he was never going to get to it, anyhow, not this afternoon, not even this day.

He had reached the shadowed side of a rundown outbuilding beyond the saddlery, paused to take stock, catch his breath, watch, listen and wait for Clyde Carter out there, slumped in a chair, sleeping off a sore head, to stir and settle again, when a movement way ahead of him, far side of the rooming-house, caught his eye and held his attention.

Somebody in no big hurry to be seen, he thought, peering deeper; somebody taking more than a fair helping of care to go about his business and stay hidden while he did it. Somebody, he thought again on a slap of his lips, a push of his hat, who looked and moved very like—

But by then it was too late to be sure of anything save being flung back against the building by the sheer force of an explosion, blinded in the whoosh and surge of flame, flying timbers, burning flotsam, then grovelling in the swirling dirt like a dog.

The silence of hours had been shattered in seconds.

Fifteen

It was a sweat-soaked, dust-caked Barney Todds who finally pulled Rawlegs from a pile of splintered, smouldering timbers, rolled him through the dirt and dragged him, coughing and spluttering, into the shade at the back of Miras Coutts' store.

'Goddamnit,' wheezed the storekeeper through a billowing of black smoke, 'who the hell did that? What's the damage, anybody see?'

'I'll tell yuh who did it,' groaned Rawlegs, smothering his face in his bandanna. 'I seen him. Oh, yes, I seen him.'

'McAdams,' said the blacksmith. 'Gotta be.'

Miras Coutts slid to the alley that led to the main street and paused at the shadowed corner of it, glancing quickly left to right. 'Hell,' he murmured, 'will yuh look at this. . . .'

'What yuh see, Miras?' called Todds. 'Any sign of that fella? What about Miss Abi? Yuh see her?'

'Just a whole mess of folk and burned-out bits and pieces. And more than likely McAdams lifted the dynamite from my store sometime. Hell. . . .'

'Yuh see anythin' of Miss Abi, f' Cris'sake?' croaked Rawlegs.

'Hold on, will yuh. . . . Let me see. . . . Yep, I got her. Right there, Sleeks Hooper and Clyde Carter lookin' to her. She ain't injured.'

'Thank the Lord for that.'

Rawlegs struggled to his feet and followed the blacksmith to the corner of the alley.

'Simmons ain't looking one bit happy. Saddlery's burned out; Rosie's roomin'-house lookin' none too healthy; livery's in one piece.'

Coutts wiped the sweat from his face. 'Fire's out. Talk about a mess. . . . Hold it, here's Simmons steppin' to the boardwalk from the bar. Goin' to make some sorta speech.'

'All right, all right,' bellowed Simmons to the smoke-fazed and dazed townsfolk standing or wandering in the street, 'let's just simmer it down there, eh? Don't nobody get to doin' nothin', 'ceptin' on my say-so. And don't nobody think of leavin'.' The crowd had turned to face him. 'I'm still sheriff here. Still the law. Don't go f'gettin' it.'

'Then yuh'd best get to pullin' in whoever did this,' shouted a man from the edge of the smoke haze.

'And soon,' called another, 'while we still got a town still standin'.'

The crowd murmured agreement.

'What about my roomin'-house?' yelled Rosie Wragges from the far end of the street. 'Who's goin' to pay for that?'

The crowd's murmurings deepened.

'All right,' bellowed Simmons again. 'It'll all get sorted.'

'And another thing,' snapped a woman, tugging at her shawl, 'what yuh doin' with Miss Abigail there? What she done wrong, Bart Simmons? Answer me that. T'ain't right, a woman bein' treated that way.'

Voices in support gathered momentum.

'Trouble brewin' now, sure enough!' hissed Miras Coutts.

'Woman's my affair,' shouted Simmons.

'Well, mebbe she ain't much for it,' answered the woman. 'No more than I'd be, come to that!'

The crowd jeered. Simmons leered. Hooper and Carter, Abigail between them, moved closer.

Joe Heane ushered a clutch of curious bar girls back through the batwings.

Rawlegs swallowed. Where the hell was McAdams, he wondered?

'Mebbe we should snatch Miss Abi now,' said Coutts.

'You'd be dead before yuh crossed the street,' grunted the blacksmith.

A shot rang out, high and whining, from Sleeks Hooper's brandished Colt.

The crowd fell silent, backing. Simmons eased his weight to one hip.

'All right. Now yuh listen up real good. Yuh hear every word I'm goin' to say. Yuh get it once and once only.' The sheriff glared into the faces watching him. 'I got a fair idea who done all this,' he began, sweeping an arm over the devastation. 'That fella I had penned 'til this young lady here, Miss Abigail Grey, no less, took it into her head to spring him. Oh, yes, don't nobody doubt it, Miss Grey was at the back of that. I got the proof of it. She broke the law. And yuh pay a price for that in my book. Don't matter who yuh are – or how much land yuh got – law's the law.'

He paused, his gaze scanning the crowd, flitting quickly to glance at Abigail.

'Sonofabitch sure gets sparin' with the truth, don't he?' drawled Rawlegs, wiping a hand across his mouth. 'What about him tryin' to get his hands on Miss Abi? What about Moldoon? He ain't much for explainin' that, is he?'

The old man spat and went back to wondering where McAdams had hidden himself. Or perhaps he had left, disappeared into the Washback.

'So there'll be no more questionin' and queryin', yuh hear?' Simmons continued. 'We get this town cleaned up. T'day, before it's full dark. And yuh leave the law and them who gets to breakin' it to me.'

'And what about Miss Abi?' called the woman in the shawl again.

'Her of all people you can definitely leave to me!' grinned Simmons, winking at Hooper. 'No harm'll come to Miss Abi, ma'am, you can rest assured.'

'None had better, Bart Simmons,' scowled the woman, 'otherwise yuh'll have me to answer to.'

'Wouldn't fancy that!' mocked a man in the crowd.

Rawlegs spat and scuffed a boot into dirt.

'No sign of McAdams,' hissed the blacksmith.

'Long gone, I shouldn't wonder,' quipped Coutts. 'Mebbe he's headed out to the homestead. Mebbe that's what we should all do, eh? Get out there before Moldoon rides in and it's too damned late—'

The three men in the alley craned forward at the sound of approaching riders, the beat of hoofs, swinging jangle of tack, creaking leather. The crowd fell silent. Simmons took a step for a broader view of the street. Hooper and Carter shifted their attention from Abigail who tossed her hair across her shoulders and stared intently in the direction of the deepening pound of hoofs, the thickening cloud of dust.

The woman in the shawl folded her arms and pursed her lips. 'Now what?' she huffed.

'Trouble,' said a man, coming to her side. 'That's all we ever get these days.'

A young boy, arms waving, hair flying, eyes wide in his head, raced down the street ahead of the riders. 'It's Stove Moldoon!' he yelled at the top of his voice. 'Stove Moldoon and a dozen men along of him!'

The riders thundered from the trail to the outskirts of town without breaking pace, their faces masked against the swirl of dust and dirt, mounts lathered and already steaming. Moldoon rode at their head, his gaze tight and fixed, shifting with what seemed barely a passing interest over the chaos of the explosion, the fire, the still drifting smoke.

Not until they were deep into the street and the townsfolk falling back to the boardwalks, did Moldoon raise an arm to slow the pace and finally bring the riders to a standstill at the steps to the saloon where Simmons, a broad, ingratiating grin breaking at his lips, stepped forward to greet them.

'Right on time, just as I figured yuh would be,' he smiled. 'And yuh been scorchin' some dirt there by the look of it.'

Moldoon pulled aside his dust mask. 'Small fry to what yuh been doin' here!' he growled. 'Just what the hell's goin' on?' He gathered the reins as his mount bucked. 'And just what, would yuh mind tellin' me, is Miss Grey doin' here?'

'Bein' held against her will,' shouted the woman in the shawl. 'Ask Simmons. He'll tell yuh.'

The crowd murmured and began to stir. Abigail continued to stare and stayed silent.

'That a fact?' scowled Moldoon.

'No, it ain't,' snapped Simmons. 'That woman there's been involved—'

'Where's that troublemaker? The one they call McAdams? Yuh holdin' him yet?' Moldoon's eyes flashed angrily. 'Don't look to have much in the way of a jail, do yuh?'

'Let me tell yuh what's been happenin' here,' began Simmons, beginning to sweat.

'Later,' said Moldoon irritably. 'I ain't in the mood right now.' He gestured to the riders at his side. 'See to it. Yuh got a free hand. Do what's necessary. I'll be in the bar.'

It was then, as the three men closest to Stove Moldoon nodded and drew aside their masks, that Rawlegs croaked deep in his throat, gripped Miras Coutts's arm and felt the blood drain thin as cold creek water from his cheeks.

'You all right?' frowned the storekeeper.

'No, I ain't,' hissed the old man. 'I ain't one miserable bit all right. Yuh see what's ridden in there? Take a good look. Them's ghosts.'

Sixteen

'Didn't get to seein' too much of 'em that day – wouldn't be here to tell it if I had – but I sure as hell seen enough. Oh, yes, I seen it all, just as it was. That's them: Blatch, Riff Stevens, Crazy Man Moon. The men who did for Sam Pooley. You don't forget faces like that.'

Rawlegs leaned back on the building in the shaded alley, closed his eyes for a moment and licked his lips. 'Never thought to see the scum again,' he murmured to the watchful gazes of Miras Coutts and Barney Todds.

'And now Moldoon's recruited 'em to his payroll,' said the blacksmith.

'Rats runnin' with rats, ain't it?' croaked Rawlegs on a dry, stinging throat. 'What matters is they're here and that can mean only one thing by my reckonin'. . . .'

Two shots rang out, high and screeching over the hot afternoon. 'What the hell,' hissed Todds, easing along the alley for a view of the street. 'One of 'em's struttin' out there, showin' who's boss.'

'That'll be Blatch,' said Rawlegs.

'Wild-eyed one with the scar across his cheek—'

'That's Stevens.'

'He's clearin' the street.'

'What about Miss Abi?' grated Coutts.

'She's just standin' there, Clyde Carter, Hooper and Simmons side of her, that other one – Crazy Man Moon – watchin' 'em, turnin' a blade through his fingers.'

'He grinnin'?' asked Rawlegs.

'He's grinnin'.'

Rawlegs pushed himself away from the wall. 'Time I was movin',' he said, spitting into the dirt, rubbing his hands together. 'Go round up my mount back of the bar there, get m'self back to the spread.'

'To the spread?' frowned Coutts. 'What about Miss Abi? What we goin' to do about her? Can't just leave her.'

'And we can't just go walkin' up to her, tippin' our hats and escortin' her home, can we? Don't figure we'd get too far! No, I gotta find McAdams. Got to get to him, hear what he's for doin'.'

'We're with yuh,' said the storekeeper, slapping a hand on his thigh. 'Ain't we, Barney?'

'Well—' began Todds.

'Let's move, while we still got legs!'

The three men slid away from the alley like shadows.

Joe Heane moved carefully, slowly behind his bar; no sudden movement, nothing to draw attention; just keep it easy, steady. Another three steps and the gun would be there, in his hand, and then tucked neat and tidy in the folds of the apron.

Time for using the piece would come later.

He paused, waited a moment, his gaze narrowing on Stove Moldoon seated at the corner table, Miss Abigail facing him, Simmons to one side, and the three new gunslinging sidekicks spread about the bar like so much trail-dusted trash.

No accounting for fellows like that, he thought, looking closer, especially not if they were who he reckoned them to be: the three who had ridden through Resolute on the day of the shooting of Sam Pooley. Fellows of their type were not to be trusted.

He took another step towards the gun on the shelf beneath the bar.

'Sorry to see it's turned out this way, Miss Grey,' Moldoon was saying, his stare unblinking on Abigail's face. 'Shame we didn't talk sense when we had the chance, before the bodies started piling up – and before that fella, McAdams, showed his face.'

'Mr McAdams is only doing—' began Abigail.

'Oh, I'm sure he is, miss – just bein' a good friend, eh? Yeah, well, I got other notions about Mr McAdams.'

'If you're suggesting—' began Abigail again.

'I ain't suggestin' nothin', miss,' drawled Moldoon, pouring a generous measure of whiskey to his glass. 'I'll handle Mr McAdams my way. Meantime, we'll get to the details of our business. . . .'

'Later, Mr Moldoon,' said Abigail, coming to her feet, dusting the folds of her skirts dramatically. 'Right now, I'm in need of a wash, somewhere to freshen up.' She glanced witheringly at Simmons. 'It's been a long, tiresome day.'

'Sure,' smiled Moldoon. 'You – barman – get Miss Grey a room. Put it on my bill. Take your time, miss, within reason, that is. I ain't for bein' in town longer than is necessary. You understand?' He nodded, the smile broadening.

Abigail returned the smile and headed through the gathering of bar girls to the stairs to the private rooms.

Damn, thought Joe Heane, following in the woman's steps. The gun would have to wait.

Abigail Grey had passed from Moldoon's sight before he ordered Simmons to post one of his men on the landing. 'I don't want that woman goin' no place.' Then, summoning Blatch closer, he murmured, 'I want McAdams as dead as he can ever get as soon as yuh can, yuh understand? No mess. No delay. I wanna be out of this town by noon tomorrow. Not a minute later.'

'Sorry about this, Miss Abi,' whispered Joe Heane, pushing open the door to the room. 'Not a deal I can do about it right now. But if I get the chance—'

'Don't put yourself about, Mr Heane,' said Abigail, stepping over the threshold to the airless, shadowed space. 'I quite understand, and I shall be quite all right, I assure you.' She looked anxiously over the man's shoulder, then beckoned him to her. 'If you could get a message to Rawlegs somehow. . . .'

'Do my best, miss.'

'If you could just tell him' – she hesitated, biting at her lip – 'just tell him I've changed my mind.'

'Just that?' asked Heane.

'Just that.'

'I reckon I read yuh aright, miss. Just leave it with me,' smiled Heane. 'Meantime,' he added, lowering his voice, 'yuh goin' to have company standin' guard on yuh. Sleeks Hooper's on his way.

Watch him. He's got a nasty turn of mind when the mood takes. Keep him this side of the door.'

Abigail grinned tamely, passed into the room, closed the door behind her and leaned back with a long, shuddering sigh.

Had she made the right decision after all, she wondered? But even if she had – even if she was following her instincts now and dismissing her fear and caution – how could she possibly bring it all to a satisfactory, not to say bloodless, conclusion?

She shuddered again at the sound of the scuff of a boot outside the door. Sleeks Hooper in position. No chance there of a quick getaway. But would that, anyway, be the wisest move? Perhaps if she were to wait, watch, trust that Joe Heane could get her message to Rawlegs, that McAdams had not ridden out. . . .

She crossed the room to the window where the drapes were drawn tight against the glare, twitched them apart for a view of the street below, and turned ice-cold at the sound at her back, the hand that reached over her shoulder, closed the drapes again and slid away like the reach of a tendril.

'Best not draw attention to ourselves, miss,' said the voice.

'He ain't here,' announced Miras Coutts, easing his saddle-sore backside to a chair on the veranda of the Pooley homestead. 'Ain't here now and ain't been here for some time. So, my guess'd be—'

'He's either still in town or close to it,' said Barney Todds, scanning the paddock. 'We goin' to stay, or move on?'

'We stay,' said Rawlegs. 'Leastways, I'm stayin' for

now. Somebody's gotta watch this place. Wouldn't put it beyond Moldoon to have some of his boys ride in.' His voice faded. 'Yeah,' he croaked on, 'scumbags like Blatch, Riff Stevens and Crazy Man Moon. They know their way, sure enough. Know every yard of it. Ride here just like they did on that day. . . .'

'Ain't no point in goin' back on that score, is there?' said the blacksmith. 'Done now, ain't it? Ain't nothin' goin' to change things.'

'Know somethin'?' smiled Rawlegs. 'You're right. 'Course you are. But that don't mean to say there ain't no retribution due, does it? I sit here long enough, 'til mebbe sun-up, and them rats'll be here, just know they will. And when they show up—'

'Yuh all talk there, Rawlegs,' snapped Coutts. 'Yuh mean well, ain't sayin' yuh don't, and I'm with yuh, but yuh wouldn't stand a half a chance, would yuh? Any one of them three would put yuh down in seconds. Fact – and yuh know it. No, what we gotta do is look to Miss Abi. Stay here if yuh like, but I figure for Barney and me best servin' the lady back in town. That's where she is: that's where we should be. What yuh say?'

'Talkin' on like we are; ridin' round in circles . . . damn it, I'm beginnin' to wonder—'

Barney Todds' words lodged in his throat like rocks at the sight of a handful of riders, Clyde Carter and Hank Speak leading them, as they veered in a swirl of dust from the main trail and pounded towards the paddock.

'Don't look like we're goin' no place, does it?' groaned Coutts. 'In fact, I'd reckon for us bein' truly corralled.'

'Shut yuh belly-achin' there, Miras Coutts,'

growled Rawlegs, slapping his lips, 'and shift yuh butt off this porch and back there into the home. Same goes for you, Barney. We're goin' to make a stand!'

'We're goin' to what?' choked Coutts.

'Make a stand!' Rawlegs' tired eyes gleamed. 'Yessir! Just that! Heck, we got enough ammunition, spare guns too back there to hold out for . . . for as long as it takes, damn it! Now, come on, let's move before them vermin ridin' in get to realizin' this place ain't quite as peaceful as it looks. This is goin, to be war – and I'm declarin' it!'

Seventeen

Abigail Grey had turned quickly, her thoughts already in a turmoil, at the sound of the voice at her back. 'Mr McAdams!' she gasped on an intake of breath and an almost painful swallow. 'How—?'

The man eased away, raising a hand to urge silence as he moved to the door, listened for a moment, then rejoined Abigail at the window.

'We ain't got long,' he murmured, his gaze dark and steady. 'I fancy for Moldoon's patience wearin' thin very soon. You still for makin' a go of that spread of yours, miss, or yuh goin' to sell out?'

'I'm stayin',' said Abigail with a toss of her hair. 'I was beginnin' to have my doubts, but now—'

'That's all I need to hear, miss. There ain't the time for more.' McAdams raised his hand again for silence, listened, waited. 'Seems like Moldoon's recruited some unsavoury types. Yuh seen 'em?' The woman nodded. 'Same three as shot Sam.'

'How did you know that?' hissed Abigail.

'Long story. We'll get to it later. Meantime. . . .' McAdams was at the door again, waiting a moment, then beckoning the woman to his side. 'Time we moved,' he whispered. 'I want you to open that door and get the fella posted there into the room. You can do that?'

'Temptation?' smiled Abigail. 'It's my speciality, remember?'

'So it is,' grinned McAdams. 'So let's do it. Yuh leave the rest to me.'

'What about—' began Abigail.

'Just do as I say, when I say it. Move. Now!'

Abigail swung her hair into her neck, patted it into place, ran her hands down the folds of her skirt and took a deep breath. 'Right,' she murmured, and reached for the doorknob.

She opened the door slowly, carefully, conscious of McAdams melting into the shadows along the stretch of wall. She paused, wondering then if she should step into the gap or wait for Sleeks Hooper to make a move.

Five, ten seconds ... it seemed to Abigail like minutes before the sidekick stirred himself and slid half into the room.

'Yuh goin' some place, miss?' he asked, his eyes already gleaming.

'I was rather hoping you'd tell me that,' smiled Abigail. Her gaze hovered. 'Or perhaps there isn't the time,' she added on a purr.

Hooper waited, the gaze moving over her, a grin spreading on his wet, shining face. 'Always make the time, miss,' he said, sliding the other half of him into the room, the door closing behind him on his gentle push. 'Man who can't make time—'

McAdams's hands sprang from the darkness like claw-winged bats; fast, soundless, flashing as if in flight to settle in a throttling grip on Hooper's throat. The sidekick croaked, his hungry gaze bulging to a sudden stare, struggled for a moment to turn, but had neither the strength nor will to shake off the grip.

Abigail watched wide-eyed, backing to the wall, as Hooper's body weakened, the legs buckling, feet splaying. She shuddered for a moment at the concentration on McAdams's face, the rippling, white-knuckled hold on Hooper's throat.

The man was sprawled unmoving on the floor in less time, it seemed, than it had taken for Abigail to catch her breath.

'Stay close,' said McAdams, stepping over the body.

Abigail followed, not daring to look down at the dead man's staring eyes.

Stove Moldoon's insistence on a 'bottle of the best' for Blatch and his gunslinging partners to 'oil their necks' on – 'none of the cheap Washback varnish you're stackin' back of the bar there' – was to be the lucky break McAdams had been praying on.

Joe Heane, muttering his opinions on a waste of good liquor well below his breath and out of earshot of the bar, had been obliged reluctantly to climb the stairs to his storeroom at the far end of the corridor, unlock the door and rummage among his supplies for the 'cheapest of the best'.

He was still muttering when he felt the silent, looming presence at his back and turned to stare into the faces of McAdams and Abigail Grey.

'How the hell yuh get in, mister?' he croaked, almost dropping the bottle clutched in his hand.

'Front bar, earlier on,' whispered McAdams. 'Can't

leave the same way. That stores door back of you open on stairs to the rear?'

'Sure does,' said Heane.

'Be obliged if we could put it to use.'

'My pleasure,' grinned Heane. 'But what about—'

'There's a dead body, room five. Stall findin' it as long as yuh can – and leave this door unlocked, will yuh? Fancy I might need it again.'

'Yuh got it,' said Heane, watching McAdams lead Abigail to the alley and the hitched mount standing in the shadows.

The bar-keeper glanced at the label on the bottle in his hand. Darn sight better quality whiskey than the scumbags deserved. Still, he thought, hurrying back to the corridor, who could say, it might be their last.

'That's goin' to be far enough, Clyde. Yuh stay right where yuh are. Not one step closer.'

The threatening probe of the shotgun barrel from the window of the homestead, the sound of Rawlegs' voice, the shadowed shapes, glint of the light on other guns, were more than enough to bring the town riders to a slithering dust-swirling halt at the corral.

Clyde Carter slid carefully, watchfully, from his mount and stepped ahead of the others. 'Bein' a mite foolish there, ain't yuh, old-timer?' he called, his gaze narrowing against the fierce glare of approaching sunset. 'Yuh ain't plannin' on shootin' this out, are yuh? How many yuh got back there? McAdams with yuh?' The man rolled his weight to one hip. 'Ain't no need for this, is there?'

'Sonofabitch!' growled Rawlegs to himself, tightening his grip on the stock of the gun. 'See yuh in Hell first.'

'Mebbe we should ease up here some,' said Miras Coutts, watching the paddock from another window.

'Yuh gettin' cold feet?' grumbled Rawlegs. 'Yuh back off now if you're sweatin' that bad.'

'Will yuh cool it, pair of you?' said the blacksmith from the side of the open door. 'Let's hear what them scum gotta say for themselves.'

'What's the deal, Clyde?' called Rawlegs.

'No deal. This ain't a dealin' situation. All simple and straightforward enough. Moldoon wants this property looked to 'til him and Miss Abigail are all through with their business.'

'Well, now, does he?' scoffed Rawlegs. 'This ain't his spread to look to, is it, and he ain't the one to go givin' orders concernin' it, is he? And you, Clyde Carter, and them rag-bag varmints yuh got sittin' back of yuh there, surely ain't the man to be lookin' to nothin', nowhere, 'specially not here.' He snorted. 'Yuh got two minutes, just that, to mount up and ride out, yuh hear? Two minutes. Any longer and you're dead where yuh stand.'

'Hell,' swallowed Coutts, 'he ain't goin' to take that.'

'I ain't foolin' none,' said Rawlegs. 'I've had it up to here with these spread-bustin', land-snatchin' no-gooders who figure all they gotta do—'

'Watch him, he's movin',' murmured Barney Todds, flexing his hold on a Winchester. 'Turnin' now. I wouldn't trust Clyde Carter further than—'

Carter swung round to face the homestead, a Colt already blazing in his hand, Hank Speak and the others joining in the barrage of fire from their saddles, the mounts circling, bucking, snorting on the sudden mayhem.

Rawlegs whooped and roared the shotgun into action, at the same time ducking instinctively against the splintering crash of shots as they peppered the homestead's veranda and walls.

Barney Todds crooked the Winchester into his hip and let it rage into life, the lead spraying among the riders like a freak hailstorm. He grinned as one of the men hit the paddock with a thud and another, bleeding at the shoulder, lost control of his mount and was thrown.

The storekeeper shuddered and blinked at a shattering of glass and crockery, the whining singe of flying lead.

'Damnit, Miras,' yelled Rawlegs, 'if yuh can't aim straight then yuh sure as hell get to reloadin'!' And he threw the shotgun into his arms, at the same time grabbing a rifle. 'Now come and get it, yuh rats!'

Somewhere a cooking pot was sent skimming across the floor. A chair cracked and collapsed in a heap of split timbers. A half-empty bottle of whiskey was shattered to a shower of shining shards of glass; a bullet ricocheted across a plate and buried itself in the ceiling.

'Some of 'em are pullin' back!' shouted Coutts as another rider hit the dirt.

'Where's Carter?' called Todds to no answer save another whine of shots.

'Hank Speaks is hit. He's ridin' out!'

'Darnit, they got about as much backbone among 'em as—' Rawlegs voice cracked as if someone had taken an axe to it. He fell back against the table, dropping the rifle, one hand gripping the top of his leg where the blood was already bubbling. 'Sonofa-goddam—' he moaned, crashing to the floor.

Barney Todds swung to his right, the Winchester kicking hot and fierce in his grip as he released a stream of shots that threw Clyde Carter from the veranda, down the few steps to the dirt and across the paddock like a twist of paper caught in a whirl-wind.

'Hell,' groaned Coutts again, blinking on the smoke, the cordite, the clouding dust.

'Yeah, just that,' growled Rawlegs from the floor, the blood still bubbling at his leg. 'We about all through here?'

'All through,' sighed Todds. 'For now.'

Eighteen

McAdams, with Abigail Grey mounted at the back of him, had cleared Resolute on the rarely used, deserted trail that swung out far to the northern reaches of the drylands before turning again for the Washback.

They had ridden in silence, McAdams concentrated on the track, Abigail, still in a daze of shapes, voices, faces and places, clinging tightly to him against the pace of the mount, the gathering dusk seeming to be full of plunging shadows and a darkness that was real enough when they finally rounded the bluff and headed into the homestead paddock.

'Goddamn it, Miss Abi, we didn't have no choice,' Rawlegs had protested, doing his best to hide the pain of his wound while he apologized for the state of the place. 'If we hadn't made a stand against them scumbags, there just ain't no tellin' what they might have gotten to.'

And it had taken much of the rest of that evening until the onset of the full night before Abigail had calmed the old man, dressed his wound and assured him he had done exactly the right thing and that she would have done the same had she been there.

'That mean we're fightin' on, miss?' Rawlegs had asked from the brink of an exhausted sleep.

But the old man was snoring contentedly long before Abigail had said all she wanted.

'Borrowed time, ain't it? Can't say other. Moldoon ain't goin' to take all this lyin' down, is he? Yuh seen the vermin he's put in his pay – them three who shot Sam? You seen 'em, McAdams? They're right there in town.' Miras Coutts sniffed loudly and stared despairingly into the night. 'Like I say, borrowed time. That's all we got.'

'Well,' said Barney Todds, from the edge of the lantern glow at the homestead door standing open to the veranda, 'what yuh reckon, mister? Miras here right, is that all we really got – borrowed time?'

'Surely Moldoon's men won't ride out here tonight, will they?' frowned Abigail, stepping from the living-room.

'No sayin' to it, is there, miss?' said Coutts. 'Moldoon ain't exactly known for his patience. If he's as riled as I figure him for bein' over the state of things in town, and now you gettin' away from him, McAdams here interferin' again – well, I'd say Stove Moldoon's company ain't exactly the choicest to be keepin'! Wouldn't like to be standin' in Sheriff Simmons's boots, and that's for sure.'

'Perhaps I should –' began Abigail.

'No, Miss Abi, don't you go even thinkin' it,' interrupted the blacksmith. 'Times like this, when the nerves get frayed and there don't seem to be a deal else save the waitin' and wonderin' – that's just what Moldoon wants. Just the sort of thing he preys on.'

'Sun-up,' said McAdams from the shadows. 'It'll be sun-up when they get to it again.'

'You crossed the paths of them three gunslingers before, mister?' asked Coutts carefully, his gaze narrowing. 'Yuh have, haven't yuh? I can feel it in my bones.'

Abigail smoothed the folds of her skirt. 'Well, it hardly matters, does it?' She smiled quickly. 'It isn't going to change them being there, and it certainly isn't going—'

'I crossed 'em.'

McAdams blew a thin wisp of cigar smoke from the darkness, his eyes gleaming. 'Long back, out Lacarta way, Mexican border. Me and Captain Pooley—'

'Sam?' gasped Abigail.

'Sam Pooley had seen 'em before?' croaked Todds.

'He had. Like I say, we crossed 'em at Lacarta. Run in with some bandits that way: Blatch, Riff Stevens and Crazy Man Moon were along of 'em. Captain Pooley, myself and our platoon, we broke up the gang, but Blatch and his partners rode clear, Blatch bein' wounded bad. Said as how he'd one day settle it with the captain. Said he'd hunt him down if it was the last thing he did.'

'And the sonofabitch did just that,' murmured Coutts.

McAdams blew another wisp of smoke. 'Sam had been hearin' talk for some while that Blatch and his boys were rovin' the territory. Only a matter of time, he figured, before they wandered into Resolute.' He looked away into the night. 'Told me all this in the letter he wrote. Too damned late by the time I was readin' it.'

'And now Moldoon's put the scumbags on his payroll,' said Todds. 'He must know who they are, know they shot Sam.'

'He knows,' grunted McAdams.

'Hell,' croaked Coutts. 'What sort of vermin is it can come back to where they shot a man, knowin' full well as how the woman the fella was goin' to wed. . . .' The storekeeper gulped on his words. 'Darnit, what am I sayin' here, miss? I never meant. . . .'

Abigail's gaze darkened, a fine drift of sweat glistening on her upper lip. 'They should hang,' she said coldly. 'Somebody should make certain they die.' And then she turned and strode back into the house, slamming the door shut behind her.

McAdams's stare gleamed again from behind another wisp trailing of smoke.

Barney Todds watched a curl of his breath drift like a thin white veil on the chill dawn air. The light in the sprawl of the long, empty lands to the east was still faint, no more than a vague grey smudge across the fading night. It would be another full hour to the first spill of sunlight. Time enough, he reckoned, for the man to be clear of the Washback and hidden deep in the shadows wherever he found them.

He shifted uneasily. Hard to say if he should approach the fellow or let him be. McAdams was not for messing with, especially not at this hour, in the half light and the silence with his resolve very obviously set and determined and all his concentration on the job of saddling up and riding out. Not the time to argue a point, that was for sure.

Even so . . . damn it, why should the fellow shoulder this alone? True, he had been Sam Pooley's best friend, stood to him and along of him through more scrapes and skirmishes than he maybe cared to recall, but that had been long back at a time when scrapes and skirmishes were a way of life, done by the book. And they were paid for it!

This was now, in a two bit, one-eyed town, where the sheriff was corrupt and the life not much of a deal save for dirt, dust and the sprawling emptiness of the Washback, and men like Moldoon figured on most of it being theirs by right, fair means or foul, usually the latter.

Best thing Miss Abigail could do was maybe sell up, take whatever she could raise on the spread and go build herself a decent life somewhere out in Colorado, or Missouri, wherever the fancy took.

Sure, and just who was he convincing with such yellow-belly talk? Did he really think Miss Abi would do that? Hell, did he really think there was a man hereabouts could look himself in the eye and *let* her do that? Least of all Sam Pooley's best friend.

And if Sam could look down right now, he would be seeing no more, no less, than he would have expected and done himself had the need arisen. He would not be arguing. Neither should anyone else.

Even so . . . there would be Blatch, Riff Stevens and Crazy Man Moon back there in Resolute; three guns waiting for only one target. It was still something to ask the fellow to go it alone.

'Yuh all decided there now, Mr Todds?' said

McAdams quietly, his back to the shadowed veranda where the blacksmith waited.

Todds swallowed and rubbed a hand over his stubbled chin. 'I was just kinda wonderin' here—'

'Know exactly what yuh were wonderin', Mr Todds, and I'm obliged for your concern, but it won't be necessary. I figure I can handle this.'

'Well, I wasn't doubtin' that. Hell, man, yuh gotta remember who'll be waitin' on yuh out there. And that ain't countin' on the others standin' to Moldoon and Simmons. I'd be more than willin'—'

'I'm sure yuh would,' said McAdams, mounting up, 'and don't think I'm not grateful. Way I figure it, though, be as well if yourself and Mr Coutts looked to Miss Abi and Rawlegs. Get this place cleaned up some, eh?' He reined his mount to the Washback and the trail into town. 'You tell Miss Abi I'll be back for supper.'

'That a promise?' called the blacksmith.

'That, Mr Todds, is a fact!'

Nineteen

Joe Heane listened to the slow, painful tick of the saloon bar clock, waited for the drifting smoke to clear, and squinted on the gloom – half lantern glow, half first light – for the position of the hands. Just after five, he noted, leaning back in the chair at the corner table. Give it another hour at most. McAdams would not be for leaving it longer.

He rested a hand on the table, one finger tapping instinctively, silently to the measure of his concentration on the faces of the three men seated in the shadows fronting the batwings.

Riff Stevens had seemed to be sleeping for the past hour. Sure, mused Joe, had *seemed* to be. About as asleep as a basking rattler waiting for its next meal! Would only take a shadow to shift and the man's eyes would be open, cold as chilled steel, and a hand settling on the inlaid bone butt of his Colt faster than a fly to dead meat. Chances were, Joe reckoned, that the man had never truly slept in years.

Same might be said for his partner, the one they called Crazy Man Moon. His eyes, the palest shade of blue, shot through with ice, were never still. They flitted like moths looking for a light, never settled; moved on, missed nothing. Wild, restless eyes, thought Joe. Not hard to see how he came by the nickname Crazy Man. He probably was.

The oldest of the trio, the one they only ever referred to as Blatch, had definitely slept some in the last hour; leastways he had dozed. Maybe he needed to at his age. Maybe he had been so long staying a step ahead of the law or dodging the next vengeful bullet that sleep was no problem. Or maybe he simply trusted to his partners staying awake. Or knew full well they were too fearful not to.

Few words had been exchanged between the men since Moldoon's anger at the loss of Abigail Grey, the discovery of Hooper's body, the 'bare-faced sono-fabitch audacity of that fella, McAdams', and Sheriff Simmons's 'incompetent, mule-headed bunglin' ', had finally subsided on Blatch's assurance that McAdams would be dead before noon.

'That the same McAdams we crossed out Lacarta way along of Sam Pooley?' Crazy Man had drawled.

'One and the same,' Stevens had yawned.

'Well, we sure as hell owe him some, don't we? And you can bet your boots to a dollar he'll come ridin' in here at first light, babe to a slaughter.' Crazy Man had dribbled on his tittering. 'We goin' to be waitin' on him, Blatch? That what yuh thinkin'? Turkey shoot at sun-up, that what we got?'

Joe Heane's tapping finger lay still as he squinted again through the gloom for a sight of the hands on the saloon bar clock.

Alvin Johnson had seen it all, right from the day they had buried Captain Pooley on Boot Hill. And he figured he would see the last of it too, probably before Miss Martins tolled the bell for school way things were going – always assuming Miss Martins had the stomach for school when it came to it, that is. Not that he would be attending. No chance, not on a day like today.

Alvin hurried on through the deserted, half-lit, still sleeping town, threading his way silently between the cluttered crates, barrels and timbers at the back of the main street buildings.

Only one place to be when the showdown came, he reckoned: top of the livery at the open loading bay. See the whole street from there. And with Mr Todds being out of town, otherwise engaged on the Pooley spread, getting up to the bay and staying there would be no problem.

Almost as good as being a part of it all with a view like that, thought Alvin. No saying, of course, as to who would make the first move. The gunslingers were holed-up in Mr Heane's saloon bar and were in no hurry to move. No hint yet of McAdams being in town. Sheriff Simmons was staying low. Maybe he was not for tangling, leastways not till the shooting was done. Most other folk would probably do likewise. But not Alvin Johnson! Nossir, there was history being made here today, and he was not for missing it.

He skirted the devastation at the jail and slipped quickly through the shadows at the saddlery. Majority of Resolute residents were still sleeping or perhaps staying well clear of the day coming up. Well, choice was theirs, of course, but when it came. . . .

Alvin halted right where he was – about to cross

the short run of open ground to the livery – conscious now of another presence. He swallowed, felt a sweat gathering chill as ice in his neck. Oh, yes, there was somebody here, sure enough. He could see the gleam of the eyes in the shadows, feel them watching him. Somebody he had seen before.

'That you, Mr McAdams?' croaked Alvin, on a throat that suddenly seemed to be no part of him.

'Mornin', boy. About early, ain't yuh?'

'I was kinda figurin' . . .' began Alvin, his voice thinning to a whisper as he peered for a face to the voice. 'That's to say. . . .'

'Yuh spare me a minute or so of yuh time?' asked the voice.

'Why, sure. I guess I don't plan on bein' no place 'til. . . .' Alvin swallowed on the cracked throat. 'I mean. . . . Well, you just name it, Mr McAdams.'

'Three fellas waitin' in the saloon back there. Yuh heard about them?'

'Oh, sure, I heard, and I seen 'em too. They're in there, mister. Talk is as how they're waitin' on you.'

'I reckoned as much. Well, I ain't one for bein' impolite, so mebbe you could just let them fellas know I'm in town and I'll be with 'em just as soon as I've looked to my horse here. Wouldn't want 'em to think I hadn't shown or was keepin' 'em waitin', would I?'

Alvin's next swallow took an age to clear his windpipe. 'I – I guess not,' he stuttered, the sweat trickling into his back.

'You do that for me, boy? What's yuh name?'

'Alvin, sir. Alvin Johnson.'

'Well, now, Alvin, you just cut along there, deliver that message and I'll be real obliged.'

The boy hesitated as if about to say something, step forward, step back, collapse in a dead faint, but could only gulp and blink violently.

There was no one in the shadows by the time his eyes were fully open again.

Sheriff Bart Simmons needed a wash, a shave, a change of shirt, a decent meal – a fast horse, if he could lay his hands on one – but opted instead for another long swig from the half-empty bottle of whiskey.

He grimaced at the fury of the taste, shook his head, and rubbed a hand over the dust-smeared window of his cluttered, fire-charred office. Hell, this was some mess, he thought, his vision swimming. Sleeks Hooper dead, Clyde Carter shot out at the Pooley spread; Marty Neale dead, Ben Norton cut up to no good use; Moldoon breathing down his neck, and now three roughneck gunslingers sitting it out in Joe Heane's bar waiting on the hour when they could line up there on the boardwalk and spit the lead till one man lay dead in the dirt.

And it was all a whole sight too late now for him to lift a finger to stop it.

He grimaced again, squinted into the street and groaned. He should never have gone against Miss Abigail like he had; should have listened to McAdams and Rawlegs. Only thing for it now was to try to get to McAdams before he hit town; warn him what was waiting; maybe stand to him if he could sober up soon enough.

He had the whiskey bottle in his hand again when he stepped closer to the window and rubbed at the pane.

Now just what in hell was young Alvin Johnson doing about this early, he wondered, watching the boy hurry down the street? And just what did he think he was doing heading for the saloon like that?

He grunted. Well, here was a situation he *could* do something about. Too right he could!

Twenty

Alvin Johnson wondered if his legs really would support his body for the few yards left to reach the steps to the boardwalk fronting the saloon. And even if they did, what then? Would he still be standing when he came to face the gunmen; would he deliver his message then turn and run? Supposing Blatch and his partners had other ideas? Supposing. . . .

He was conscious for a moment of Sheriff Simmons, stumbling drunkenly from his office to the street, of him setting off as if in pursuit. Well, no time for messing with the sheriff right now, thought Alvin, hurrying on again. Mr Simmons would have to wait. There were other, far more pressing matters to attend.

Heck, some morning this was turning out to be! He had never for a second reckoned on finding himself. . . . Here were the steps, the boardwalk, the batwings.

'Whoa there, boy. Ease up, will yuh? What's the rush?'

A face, the other side of the wings. Was that Blatch? No, the one they called Stevens, his eyes narrowed but still fixed and tight in their gaze.

'I got a message for Blatch,' gulped Alvin, sweating and breathless, but with all the bravado he could summon.

The man in the bar waited a moment, his gaze hardening and probing. 'That a fact?' he drawled.

'It sure is, mister, and I ain't foolin' none.' Alvin made to mount the steps, thought better of it and took a step back to the street. 'Message is from Mr McAdams.'

The man in the bar stiffened, murmured something to someone behind him, then pushed open the 'wings and stepped into the shadowed half-light. 'Yuh seen him?' he drawled again. 'He in town?'

Alvin blinked, swallowed, sweated. 'I seen him,' he croaked, 'and he says to tell yuh he'll be with yuh just as soon as he's looked to his horse.'

'Where'd yuh see him?' said Stevens, his gaze wider and brighter. 'Show me.'

Alvin had half-turned, his mouth open, one arm lifting, when Simmons stumbled to his side.

'I'll see to this nosyin' young 'un,' he slurred. 'Just leave him to me. Shouldn't never be about this hour. Hell, boy, what yuh think yuh doin?'

'Stand aside, Simmons,' snapped Stevens. 'Boy's my concern.'

It was in this moment, with the sheriff swaying perilously, his gaze rolling, and the gunslinger moving through slow, measured steps to the street, that Alvin took to his heels.

'I ain't the concern of nobody!' he yelled, darting away between the two men, the sheriff's floundering, outstretched arms and Stevens's snatching reach, before squirming round a water butt and a crate to the narrow alley at the side of the saloon.

'Young varmint—' blustered Simmons.

Stevens pushed him aside. 'Leave it and get outa my way!' he growled, his gaze scanning the street.

'Now just you go easy there, mister,' slurred Simmons, stumbling for his balance. 'Might remind yuh I'm still the law around here, and there ain't no sonofa—'

The shots spat and screamed through the dirt like scalded rats.

Simmons finally lost his balance and crashed to the ground with a limp-bodied thud. Riff Stevens backed instinctively to the shadow, but not before a third shot had clipped the side of his boot. There was the sound of the scraping of chairs, the crash of a table to the floor from inside the saloon, a brief passage of faces across the batwings. But no one ventured beyond them.

The sheriff cursed and squirmed through the dirt like a lizard for the cover of the boardwalk foundations.

Stevens waited, gaze narrowed again, Colt drawn, before sidling towards the water butt. There was nothing to see of the shootist; no gleam of a Winchester barrel, no shape, no sounds save the echoing whine of the gunshots.

'McAdams!' he called, dodging quickly to the water butt, dropping to one knee behind it. 'Yuh hear me there? I got the measure of yuh. Best step out now before me and the boys blast yuh to Kingdom Come.'

He stiffened, watching, fingers tensing and flexing on the butt of his Colt, the faintest gleam of sweat at his lips. 'McAdams!' he called again, the sound of his voice lost on the still deserted street. 'I ain't for spinnin' this out. . . .'

'Nor me neither.'

Riff Stevens might have been aware of the sudden drift of shadow at his back, he might have sensed a soft footfall, the merest drift of breath. The sweat on his lips would almost certainly have chilled as he came slowly upright, turned and stared into McAdams's expressionless face.

'Lacarta,' murmured the gunslinger.

'Just so,' said McAdams, his Winchester levelled and steady. 'Myself and Captain Sam Pooley. Yuh recall Sam Pooley, don't yuh? Last yuh seen of him was his back, I'm told.'

Stevens's sudden jab with the Colt was the tell-tale movement that McAdams had been waiting for, the split-second of reaction that brought the rifle into roaring life again and spun the man from the water butt to a sprawled mass that twitched only once before it lay lifeless.

Sheriff Simmons vomited where he crouched.

Alvin Johnson stared wide-eyed from the depths of the alley.

There were no sounds from the saloon.

And nothing to be seen of McAdams by the time the street dirt was darkening under the stains of Riff Stevens's blood.

Stove Moldoon backed hurriedly from the upstairs window of his saloon room fronting the street, ordered the bar girl to 'Get dressed and get out' and the sidekick standing guard at the door to 'Get in here, tell me what yuh can see down there. That fella Stevens dead?'

'He's dead, boss,' said the sidekick, peering from the window.

'McAdams?' asked Moldoon.

'Don't see nothin' of him.'

'That'll be McAdams.'

The sidekick drew himself to his full height. 'Yuh want for me and some of the boys to go sort it?'

'No, no, not yet. Leave it to Blatch. This is his affair. He's got personal interest. We wait, stand back and watch. Yuh get me?'

'I get yuh,' said the man. 'Yuh figure for Blatch bein' that good?'

'Goin' to have to be, ain't he?' grinned Moldoon. 'Alternative ain't much of a prospect.'

'We got an undertaker in town if you're interested,' said Joe Heane from behind the bar. 'Could go raise him for yuh, assumin' he ain't already up and on his way. Got a real nose for business has Zachary.'

'When we want an undertaker, I'll tell yuh,' growled Blatch, watching the street from the bat-wings.

'Them mangy flies are gettin' to him,' murmured Crazy Man Moon, staring from the window. 'Riff couldn't abide flies. Had a real thing about 'em, he did.'

'Well, he ain't for complainin' now, is he?' Blatch's eyes narrowed. ' 'Stead of watchin' flies, why don't you get useful and go see if yuh can pluck the wings off that fella, McAdams?'

'Why, I'd fancy that for bein' a real pleasure, Mr Blatch,' sneered Crazy Man. 'You got any ideas where I might start? Could be anywheres by now, couldn't he?'

'You got eyes, ain't yuh?'

A nerve in Crazy Man's cheek began to pulse and

twitch, his eyes to glisten, wet and cold. 'I surely have, Mr Blatch. I surely have,' he murmured, walking slowly to the door at the back of the bar, a knife already gleaming in his hand. He paused as he drew level with Joe Heane. 'You save me a bottle of yuh best, yuh hear?' Heane nodded. 'Good,' smiled Crazy Man. 'See yuh soon.'

Blatch sighed, spat over the batwings to the boardwalk and went back to watching the flies settling like plague spots on Riff Stevens's face.

Alvin Johnson shivered. Could he, should he, summon the courage to brush away the fly that persisted in settling on his cheek, he wondered? Would anyone notice, see the movement, even though he was buried in the deepest of the alley shadows?

Sheriff Simmons was still out there. There was no saying where McAdams had disappeared to; no saying either when the two gunslingers still in the bar might make a move. One thing was for certain, they sure knew McAdams was in town. Message had been delivered loud and clear!

Alvin shivered again and licked at a line of sweat. Heck, he had seen every detail of the shooting; the look on Riff Stevens's face, that slow, piercing shift of the gleam in McAdams's gaze; the lightning flash of the fingers as the Winchester had roared into action.

He swallowed and blinked rapidly. It was one thing planning on having the best view in town of McAdams's showdown with Blatch and his sidekicks; it was something else being this close – maybe too close now he came to reckoning it.

Perhaps he could slip away from here, work his

way back to the livery. Sheriff Simmons was in no state to give a deal of chase; more likely to be concerned with his own skin and watching Blatch. McAdams needed nobody save himself.

Definitely time to move.

He took a last look at the pesky fly, decided it was settled content enough on the lid of a barrel, and rose slowly, fearfully from the depths of his cover.

Only when he was about to step clear into the alley and head for Todds' livery did he hear the creak of the saloon's back door as it opened as if to the touch of a ghost.

Twenty-One

It was a full minute before there was a shape at the half open door. At first no more than the shift of a shadow, then the darker firmness of a boot, a trousered leg, the merest glide of a body behind the reach of a hand. And then the face.

The boy swallowed a gasp as Crazy Man Moon's flitting, piercing stare seemed to settle directly on him before moving on, probing and picking at every detail of the cluttered alley.

Seconds then until the man showed more of himself, sidling through the space with all the slippery stealth and silence of a snake, one hand still clutching the knife, the other alive with flicking, flexing fingers.

Alvin swallowed another gasp and hardly dared to breathe or blink as he watched. How long before he was spotted? Or would the gunslinger keep moving, work his way to the street, the store, the livery, wherever he figured for McAdams being holed up? How long before the town got to moving? Folk had heard the shot, some may even have seen the shooting, most would get to seeing the body there in the street. Only a matter of time before Zachary sniffed out the prospect of business.

But meantime, Alvin wondered, what about McAdams? Maybe somebody should get to him to warn him that Crazy Man was on the loose. Perhaps he already knew. Perhaps he was already waiting on him clearing the back of the alley.

The man was moving on.

The door creaked back to its latch. Crazy Man waited, grinned softly to himself, threaded his way through crates and barrels and paused again in the deepest shadow. Silence.

And the silence might have held and Crazy Man reached the street had it not been for the fly that had taken such a fancy to Alvin. It buzzed angrily into flight from the lid of the barrel, climbed and swung through the light, then dived headlong into the boy's face.

It struck Alvin at the corner of his mouth, stinging with all the venom of a cactus needle. He jumped to his feet, knocking a plank to the ground, a rusty pail into the side of a crate, an empty bottle into a spin across the dirt.

Crazy Man swung round, the blade tensed and thrusting, his other hand spread over the butt of a holstered Colt, a scowl glistening in the creases of his face.

Their gazes met – the boy's wide-eyed and moon-round, frozen it seemed in startled terror; Crazy Man's as steady as the strengthening light, cold and without the merest hint of a blink for the few seconds he waited.

'What yuh doin' there, boy?' he growled. 'Yuh should be—'

Wherever Crazy Man might have thought Alvin should have been at this hour, the boy was already on his way with a sudden dive away from the cover, into the mounds of barrels and timbers, twisting, turning, in one moment striding on at his full height, in the next crouching and scuttling like some hunch-backed beetle.

Crazy Man had taken two instinctive steps to follow, when the curl of cigar smoke from the shadows beyond the crates and barrels, deep in the tumbledown remains of a leaning shack, halted him where he stood.

The gunslinger backed, his gaze focused now on the drifting smoke and the shadow, the boy forgotten in a new and very real certainty that was beginning to dawn.

'That you there, McAdams?' he hissed across the thin air. He tensed the knife in his grip; let his fingers hover over the shape of the gun butt. 'I ain't for spreadin' this out. We either deal some, or we don't. Don't fuss me none. Yuh wanna talk to Moldoon, it can be arranged. Yuh wanna turn this into some bloodbath . . . then we'll spill some blood. And if it's Lacarta and that fella Pooley that's botherin' yuh, well, life moves on, don't it? And I sure ain't one. . . .'

Crazy Man's voice droned on emptily while he moved slowly, carefully from where he had halted towards the thicker clutter of barrels.

Alvin watched, breathless and sweating, his shirt tight in a damp chill across his back. He should not be here, he thought, twitching on a shudder. He should have kept going, stumbling on to anywhere. As it was. . . .

Heck, McAdams was right there, at the shack, deep in the shadows, just waiting. No mistaking that cigar smoke, was there? He was baiting Crazy Man into making his move. All a matter of just keeping the edge. He had heard it said among the old-timers when they got to reminiscing that it was the fellow who kept his concentration and held the edge—

Which was precisely the advantage young Alvin Johnson lost in the sudden lunge as if from nowhere of Crazy Man Moon, the vicious, iron-fast grip of his fingers on Alvin's arm as he spun the boy from behind a barrel, dragged him close and had him in a locked, throttling hold across his body in a matter of seconds.

'Your move, McAdams,' tittered Crazy Man, dribbling into his stubble, settling the knife at Alvin's throat, 'and yuh'd sure as hell better make it real careful, real slow – otherwise, this young fella here is goin' to be breathin' his last to the touch of this blade.'

Alvin shuddered as the grip on him tightened, and could only gaze speechless, motionless at the sight of another drift of cigar smoke.

'Yuh hearin' me there, McAdams? I ain't long for holdin' this nosy pup, so I suggest yuh get to makin' some decisions.'

'Don't you fret none on my account, Mr McAdams!' croaked Alvin, struggling against the man's hold.

Crazy Man growled, tightened his grip, and brought the blade closer to Alvin's throat. 'I'm countin' to ten, McAdams,' he called. 'That's how long yuh got to throw down yuh guns and step out here where I can see yuh. Yuh got that? Yuh understand – to ten? And I'm countin' now. One . . . two . . . three . . . four. . . .'

Alvin struggled again, squirmed and twisted, but Crazy Man's hold only strengthened and locked.

'Five . . . six . . . seven. . . .'

The cigar smoke continued to curl from the shadowed tumbledown. Crazy Man's breath swam hot and fetid in Alvin's neck. A fly buzzed, dived and flew on. The town lay silent and lifeless.

'Eight . . . nine. . . . I just hope yuh ain't for foulin' this up, McAdams.'

Alvin summoned the last of his strength and shifted the only limb of his body not under Crazy Man's control. He raised his right foot and crashed the heel of the boot in a skin-skimming thrust down the man's shin and across his toes.

Crazy Man yelled and cursed, his grip relaxing just sufficient for Alvin to have the space to squirm again, twist, bury an elbow in the gunslinger's gut and fling himself clear of the blade and into the side of an empty crate.

'Sonofa-goddamn-bitch!' growled the man, one hand reaching for the boy, the other for his balance.

The crate toppled, Alvin with it. Crazy Man lost the knife, fumbled for his Colt, drew it and spun round to face the shack.

'Ten,' said McAdams through a slow grin, as he stepped from the shadow, the Winchester tight and levelled and roaring into life even as the sound of his voice faded.

Crazy Man fell back into the crates and barrels, spun, gazed into McAdams's face for a moment, then crashed to the dirt, his hands empty, the Colt and the blade scattered beyond reach.

'Scoot, boy, while yuh got the chance,' ordered McAdams.

Alvin needed no second telling.

'Winchester,' murmured Blatch, turning from the batwings. 'That was a Winchester. Crazy Man don't never handle a rifle.'

Joe Heane fidgeted his hands through the folds of his apron and stared without blinking into the gunslinger's pitted, sweat and dirt-stained face. What now, he wondered? That had almost certainly been McAdams's Winchester spitting its lead. So did that mean—?

'Yuh get back there, barman, and yuh see what's goin' on,' snapped Blatch, aiming a line of spittle to the spittoon. 'Yuh hear me? Do it!'

Heane rubbed his hands through a cloth, pondered his chances of reaching for the gun behind the bar, and twitched at Blatch's sudden roar.

'I said go take a look out back, damn it! Yuh deaf or somethin'?'

'Be no need for that. I can tell yuh precisely what's out back.'

Stove Moldoon glared from the top of the stairs, a sidekick hovering a step behind him.

'Yuh been watchin' from up there?' grunted Blatch.

'Back window, and I seen all I want to,' said Moldoon, taking his time to put a light to the cheroot between his teeth. 'More than enough, in fact.' He blew a thin twist of smoke. 'Yuh just lost another man, Mr Blatch. Two down, and only yourself to go.' He grinned cynically. 'Don't look good, does it?' he went on, moving to the head of the stairs. 'Almost beginnin' to look as if you've underestimated this fella; that he's got the edge over yuh. Would yuh say that, Mr Blatch? I sincerely hope not, seein' as I'm payin' good money to get this matter sorted.'

Moldoon moved slowly down the stairs, the side-kick following. 'So, Mr Blatch,' he continued, 'what are you goin' to do? I take it you are goin' to do some-thin'? And soon – because I'm beginnin' to get a mite fretful over all this, especially now I ain't got the prospect of Miss Grey as a consolation. So can we get to it, Mr Blatch? Now!'

Moldoon paused halfway down the stairs, his eyes piercing and bright behind the slip of cheroot smoke, the sidekick grinning but watchful.

Joe Heane blinked and sweated and rubbed his hands through the cloth again.

A handful of bleary-eyed, half-dressed, bar girls gathered in the gloom of the corridor fronting the upstairs rooms.

'Well, Mr Blatch, I'm waitin',' said Moldoon.

Blatch aimed another line of spittle to the spit-toon, slipped his weight to one hip and his hands to his waist. 'So am I, Mr Moldoon,' he drawled. 'So am I – and when I'm waitin' I sure as hell don't like bein' cluttered. Nossir, that I do not.'

The blaze from the Colt suddenly in Blatch's grip threw Moldoon's sidekick into the stair rail and over it and echoed round the bar like something from a haunting.

'That's better,' smiled the gunslinger. 'Now, what was it you were sayin' there? Did I miss somethin'?'

Twenty-Two

Joe Heane dropped the cloth from his sweating hands and reached shakily for the bottle of whiskey at his side. The bar girls edged fearfully to the stair rails and stared suddenly wide awake at the sprawling, bleeding body. One of them gasped, but stifled her scream.

Stove Moldoon let a wisp of smoke crawl from the corner of his mouth. 'Was that necessary?' he asked, his gaze settling on Blatch.

'I figured so,' grinned the gunslinger. 'Things were just beginnin' to get a mite out of hand. Now we all know where we stand, don't we?' The grin faded. 'It's all accordin' to my thinkin' and my way of doin'. Right? So before yuh get to reckonin' on summonin' yuh boys into action, Mr Moldoon, just ponder on what happens when I get to feelin' cluttered. Do you understand?'

Moldoon examined the cheroot and nodded. 'Whatever you say,' he murmured watchfully.

'Good,' smiled Blatch. 'Now let's get this place cleared up. You, barman, bring me that bottle yuh got there and get this body outa my sight.' He raised his head and glared at the bar girls. 'We're closed for

149

business!' he leered. 'So you just keep outa the way
'til this is done, eh? No more gawpin'. There ain't
nothin' to see. For now.'

'Might I ask—?' began Moldoon.

'No, you may not,' snapped Blatch, still gripping
his Colt as he stepped to the batwings. 'You wanna
do somethin' useful, yuh get out there to the street
and yuh tell whoever's nosyin' about to go find
McAdams and tell him I wanna meet him. Here.
Right here. And he'd sure as hell better show or I'll
begin by killin' the barman, then the girls, before
burnin' this place and the rest of this flea-mangy
town to the ground. Do I make myself clear?'

Moldoon shrugged, heeled the cheroot and
crossed to the batwings. 'Your show, Mr Blatch,' he
grinned. 'Your show.'

Alvin Johnson was within reach of crossing to the
livery when the first of the town men finally
summoned the courage to wander into the main
street and head for the saloon.

'What the hell's goin' on?' asked one striding out
at the front of the group. 'All that shootin'. . . . I hear
there's bodies everywhere.'

'One right there. That's Riff Stevens. They say
that fella, McAdams, shot him.'

'He did too,' said an old man. 'Seen it with my own
eyes. Another one dead back of the saloon.'

'That the crazy one?'

'That's him.'

'Hell, that McAdams has sure been busy.'

'Who says he's done?' grinned the old man.

'Where's the sheriff, f'Cris'sake?'

'We ain't got one – not so's yuh'd be botherin'.'

'That's Moldoon waitin' there. What's he got to say. . . .'

It took Stove Moldoon only minutes to pass on Blatch's message. 'So there yuh are,' he concluded from the boardwalk at the saloon. 'Yuh got the size of it. That's how it stands. I suggest yuh go find McAdams fast as yuh can while yuh still got a town in one piece.'

'Wouldn't have come to this if you hadn't muscled in, Moldoon,' braved a man in the crowd to a chorus of murmurs. 'McAdams ain't doin' no more than lendin' a decent hand to Miss Grey. Can't blame him for that.' The fellow stepped forward encouraged by the others. 'And if that other gunslingin' character yuh got back there cares to step—'

The single shot rang out from the batwings on an echoing crack and whine, throwing the protestor to the dirt, blood bubbling at his shoulder.

'Got yuh answer there, ain't yuh?' said Moldoon, backing slowly to the 'wings. 'Blatch ain't foolin'. Means what he says. Don't let's go makin' it worse. Just go find McAdams, damn yuh!'

Alvin gulped on a dry, parched throat and wiped the sweat from his eyes. 'Sonofa—' he began, and bit back on the curse, shaking his head at the thought of being overheard by Miss Martins, or, worse, the clipping he would get from his pa.

'Heck,' he began again, and squatted where he waited in the lean shade. So what would McAdams do now: stroll out of cover, wherever he was holed up, walk down the street, call Blatch's bluff, call him out to a showdown?

But heck, he mouthed silently, nobody living

would trust to Blatch doing anything by the code. So where did that leave McAdams? It might be as well if somehow he could. . . .

'See you're still about, boy,' came the voice with almost the same assurance and certainty it had earlier.

Alvin came slowly upright and turned to face the deeper shadows. 'Have yuh heard, Mr McAdams?' he said softly, urgently. 'Have yuh heard what Blatch is plannin'?'

'I heard.'

'Are yuh goin' to. . . .' Alvin swallowed. 'I mean, are yuh plannin' on—?'

'Fancy deliverin' another message, Alvin? Don't have to o' course. Ain't no obligation.'

'Sure, you name it, Mr McAdams.'

A drift of cigar smoke curled from the shadows. 'You scoot yourself back to the saloon – yuh got the guts for that, Alvin?'

'Ain't nobody there spooks me, Mr McAdams,' said the boy, stiffening as he licked at the sweat on his lips.

'Figured that was so,' said the man. 'Well, you get down there again, young fella, and yuh tell Mr Blatch and anybody else listenin' there as how I'll be with him in twenty minutes. At the saloon in twenty minutes. Yuh got that, Alvin?'

'I got it, Mr McAdams. At the saloon in twenty minutes.' Alvin waited a moment, blinking. 'Is that for a fact, sir?' he asked drily. 'You'll be there?'

The cigar smoke curled. 'Twenty minutes,' murmured the voice.

Blatch prowled, a slowly emptying bottle of whiskey in one hand, his Colt in the other, his eyes flitting quickly, anxiously from the slightest movement to the batwings, from the 'wings to whoever had shifted at his back or threatened to cross his path.

Moldoon had settled at a corner table, his hands flat on its surface, his gaze following Blatch's every step, passing only fitfully to the bar, the stairs, the shadowy shapes of the huddled bar girls.

Joe Heane watched the street from the bar window. The wounded man had been carted out of sight; a group of men stood watchful and tensed outside Coutts' store; another group hovered uncertainly at the funeral parlour where Zachary was already consulting the pages of his black book, a pencil poised between anxious fingers. Nobody seemed keen to go in search of McAdams.

'Any sign of the fella?' growled Blatch.

'Not yet,' said Joe, then, craning closer to the window, 'but that young pup, Alvin Johnson, is sure in a hurry headin' this way.'

Blatch thudded the whiskey bottle to a table, spun the Colt through his fingers and crossed to the batwings.

'You bein' busy again, boy?' he called, as Alvin approached the steps to the boardwalk.

The boy paused, wiped the sleeve of his shirt across his face, and blinked. 'I got a message,' he piped in the firmest voice he could muster. 'Mr McAdams says. . . .' He gulped, his throat tightening.

'Yeah,' growled Blatch, 'what's he say?'

'Mr McAdams says he'll be here, at the saloon, in twenty minutes.'

Blatch spat over the batwings. 'Well, now, ain't that just decent of him? He sure he can spare the time?' He spat again. 'You just get in here, boy, and right now. I want yuh where I can see yuh. Here!'

Alvin glanced quickly at the groups of men in the street, wiped another lathering of sweat from his face, licked his lips and stepped up to the boardwalk. He had never been inside the saloon before, never pushed open the batwings like the grown men. Heck, he thought, he just hoped Miss Martins never got to hear of it!

Stove Moldoon stared at the bar clock. Blatch listened carefully to its steady tick and watched the movement of the minute hand as if counting down the seconds. Joe Heane tried to recall when he had last wound the clock. Must have been yesterday, he reckoned. Hell, it had better have been yesterday, because if it stopped now. . . .

He smiled cheerfully at the boy stiffening himself to the shadows in the corner. No saying what Frank Johnson would be thinking when he got to hearing what his youngest had been up to.

'That clock keep correct time?' drawled Blatch, peering intently into its face.

'Always,' lied Joe Heane.

'Don't matter none, does it?' quipped Moldoon from his table. 'T'ain't hours you're interested in, is it? It's minutes.' He tapped his fingers rhythmically. 'Yuh got just seven and a half by my reckonin'.' He smiled. 'I'd figure for McAdams bein' a time-keeper, wouldn't you? I mean, him bein' a one-time military man and all that. Once knew a certain Colonel Franklin Hooper out Fort Thomson way. . . . Now, he had a way with time. Had a timepiece size of a plate he kept watchin'—'

It was the half-stifled scream of a bar girl in the corridor to the first-floor rooms that silenced Moldoon and drew the gazes of those gathered in the bar from the face of the clock to whatever was going on above them.

'Heck . . . yuh sonofa—' mouthed Alvin Johnson.

How in the name of the cauldrons of Hell, pondered Stove Moldoon.

Should have known, thought Joe Heane. The store door to the stairs out back . . . left unlocked. 'Might have figured for it,' he murmured softly.

'Don't make a meal of it, McAdams,' cursed Blatch, striding across the bar, his Colt set and levelled. 'I know you're up there. 'Course yuh are. Sneaked in the back way, eh? Well, gotta say I admire a man who gives himself an edge. Yessir. . . .' He scowled and spat across the floorboards. 'But not today, my friend. Not today. We got other things. . . .'

Somewhere in the silence and tension of that bar, with the day's fresh light at the window, creeping through the batwings and already building shadows as thick and big as headstones, a Winchester clicked, as if taking its breath, and then began to roar.

'Lacarta . . . Sam Pooley . . . the man who came to build a life on the Washback . . . the man they shot in the back. And now there's only the ghost of him.'

It was a long hour before they finally cleared the saloon bar of the smell of smoke and cordite and spilled blood, and the bodies of Blatch and Stove Moldoon's sidekick had been collected to join the others in Zachary's funeral parlour.

Only then did Joe Heane find the courage to

announce that it was 'business as usual' and 'first drinks on the house'.

Alvin Johnson drank sarsaparilla.

Twenty-Three

'That's a true match of like minds you're lookin' at there, mister. A marriage made in Heaven if ever I seen one.' Rawlegs eased his weight to the stick held firm in his hand, pushed at the brim of his hat and gazed with an expression of warm satisfaction at the wedding group gathered on the steps to the church. 'Yessir,' he added, assured that the stranger was still standing at his side. 'Best thing happened to this town in a long whiles.'

The old man slapped his lips and sighed. 'Some reckoned as how it might never come about, o' course, but not me. No way. I saw it comin', well now, let's think. . . . Must have been that very same day of the shootin'. Sure to have been. But mebbe yuh never got to hearin' of the shootin', eh? Put Resolute on the map and no mistake. Fella there – the groom, that is; McAdams by name – well, he took out them gunslingers, Riff Stevens, Crazy Man Moon and Blatch, right there, across at Joe Heane's saloon. Yuh wanna know more about that yuh wanna talk to that smart-lookin' boy there, young Alvin, at Miss Abigail's side – Mrs McAdams as is now, o' course. Yessir!

'Anyhow, McAdams said that day as how he'd be back for supper when the business in town was done – and we all knew what he meant by "business" – and sure enough, he was. Rode in to Miss Abi, m'self, Miras Coutts and Barney Todds back there at the homestead with the tellin' of the shootin' and the real good news that Stove Moldoon, land-grabbin' sonofabitch with more money than sense, had pulled back from his efforts to buy – steal more like – Miss Abi's spread and ridden out. And darn good riddance!'

Rawlegs eased his weight on the stick. 'Lucky for Moldoon, o' course, that McAdams let him go, but, like he was tellin' me later, there'd been enough blood spilled in Resolute and, in any event, he figured as how Moldoon had seen the way of things clear enough. Too right! We ain't seen hide nor hair nor heard a peep of him since.

' 'Course,' Rawlegs continued carefully, 'the other fact of the matter is that McAdams had done what he saw as right by his good friend, Sam Pooley, buried up there on Boot Hill. Stevens, Crazy Man and Blatch were worm meat, and that counted a whole lot.' He sighed. 'Only a short step from there to gettin' the town cleaned up like yuh see it today. Yessir, that two-bit, double-dealin' Sheriff Simmons hightailed it outa town faster than a rattler in a fire cracker, and we ain't seen him since neither. Got ourselves a new lawman now. As for any other loose baggage scum of the likes of Simmons hangin' on . . . well, that's all they did do: hung on 'til we kicked 'em out! No messin'! No trash, no place for trash.

'Anyhow . . . where was I, case you're still interested . . . ah, yes, Miss Abi and Mr McAdams. Well, I seen that comin' like yuh do, yuh know . . . word here, look there . . . and, hell, what a match on a spread the likes of the old Pooley place. Yessir, I figure for Mr and Mrs McAdams doin' the place proud.

'And I got m'self a sorta share in it, so to speak. Give a helpin' hand where I can, yuh know, best as this old gunshot leg'll let me – and, say, that's another story for the tellin' if you're ever passin' down the Washback trail – so Miss Abi's fixed me up real smart and snug in that bunkhouse with my own veranda and rocker. Yeah, real nice. . . .'

Rawlegs settled his hat and brushed the dust from his waistcoat. 'Well, guess I'd best get back along of the happy couple there.' He paused a moment, leaning his weight to the stick, then added, 'Never no sayin', is there, what a stranger ridin' in might be carryin' along of him – same as McAdams there, day he rode in, remember it like it was just yesterday. No, just never no sayin'.

'Anyhow, nice talkin' to yuh, mister. Enjoy yuh stay in town, and if you're ever out the McAdams's spread, you look me up, eh? Get to tellin' yuh about the time Miras, m'self and old Barney made a stand against them gunslingin' varmints Simmons and Moldoon had rustled up. Now that was just one helluva day. Don't come up that often, yuh know, but when they do. . . .'